MW00908124

Evenings Along the Stream

Evenings Along the Stream

M. David Detweiler

Stackpole Books

Published by
STACKPOLE BOOKS
Cameron and Kelker Streets
P.O. Box 1831
Harrisburg, PA 17105

Printed in the United States of America

10 9 8 7 6 5 4 3 2 1

First Edition

Library of Congress Cataloging-in-Publication Data

Detweiler, M. David.
    Evenings along the stream / M. David Detweiler. — 1st ed.
      p.   cm.
    ISBN 0-8117-0746-6
    I. Title.
PS3554.E867E94   1990
813'.54—dc20   90-9536
                                                       CIP

for Frankie and Meade

one

Furling and unfurling against the forest's shadows like a luminous, flowing angelstrand, fly fishing is the line, its undulations as spellbinding as intriguing patterns of music or the thread, everchanging, ever—subtly—repeating, of a clever tale.

You stand in the stream with the current flowing against your boots and you snap your wrist forward sending your line out before you. You whip all that line back over your shoulder as you stand watching your target-point on the waters, then accelerating your wrist you power your line forward again like cracking a whip, except flyline never snaps or even touches itself in the air—must always be smooth-looping when you hurl it.

You are throwing the line, casting the weight of the line. To help you you have a wand, a rod, through which your line passes. To catch fish you tie a practically weightless fly, or "pattern," to the end of your line by means of a spider-web-delicate length of leader, which, settling on the currents like an invisible gesture when you cast, delivers your fly so the fish can't see it's connected to anything.

Your aim is to deceive. You want the trout under the water to mistake your floating pattern for an aquatic insect, or a land insect blown off some grasses onto the brook, or if you're fishing a wet fly or a weighted nymph in the pushing flows under the surface you want the fish to think they're seeing the aquatic insect's larval or pupal stage, the kind of food that wriggles and tumbles about underwater.

You can learn the basics of this in a morning and spend the rest of your days trying to master even just some of the subtleties. It's as hard as trying to figure the truth out about somebody. It's a beautifully frustrating way to pass the time, and I'm average at it. I'm below average at it as a matter of fact, but he was good. He was an intense, successful fisherman and I imagine him, that morning, fairly bursting through the forest in his excitement.

He'd been working without rest. The President had called him back to Washington the winter before and since then he'd been toiling in the mouth of the dragon, lying and creating, building and destroying, twelve hours a day seven days a week. To be hurrying through green woods on his way to his favorite trout water he had been promising himself, shutting his eyes a long, regenerative moment at the meetings, since January.

He started downhill now, the forest thickening around him in a storm of branches as he descended. He had to stop and disentangle himself where the brush became too dense, and backtrack and go around a different way.

The stream was ahead somewhere through the trees. He couldn't see it but he could sense it—he was excited. I can see him. I can feel his exuberance as the big shoulders swing through the forest. I can see the cruel, merry eyes gliding through the tangles and hangings of brush. Carrying his rod backward to keep it from getting snagged as he bushwhacks his way through the riot of honeysuckle and briars and crawlers, he pauses—kicks the fallen treetrunk, waiting to see if a snake will slide out from under, before lifting a booted foot to step over. The smells of the forest are vivid all about him now as he descends, sharp, aromatic pine scent, perfumy honeysuckle, tart and musky dank of rotting wood. Lightly the treebranches censer last night's rainwater upon him as he shoulders them aside.

His rugged features—heavy jaw, cliff cheeks, sun-mottled skin, piercing eyes and wide, flat mouth—have not set, like cement, into that dead expression some men learn to use until it becomes all they have. He has a young face, over which emotions play as generously as changing moods on the face of a babe.

Lowering his head he hunkers to waddle through a bower of vines. The air is different now, damper. The trickle of water following beside him grows to a rivulet meandering downhill alongside him as he descends: loam-brown water flowing over outcroppings of ruddy shale and gravelly washslides of gray pebbles.

Suddenly through the trees it is there, a path of brightness, a moving, stately way, the shining and processional glide, through the forest's dark columns, of thousands of gallons of water . . .

He approached quietly, the current so clear it was like liquid light sliding by before his eyes.

Each streambottom stone, smoothed by time, cast its separate, sharp shadow in the brilliance.

The far bank was a wall of hemlocks, their dark boughs,

sagging out low over the water, seeming to sleep. Steadily the stream swept along under the slumbering boughs.

And in the brightness that was the current there were lights. Silvery and dazzling they held, as if suspended in jewel-perfect air, finning to keep in position, facing upstream.

He stood watching them, his equipment hanging from him, his eyes child-innocent.

The stream was more beautiful that morning than he had ever seen it. All was still, the forest quiet, the air washed fresh by the previous evening's rain, the silence of the current broken now and again by the soft, random cluck flowing water likes to make.

Keeping back in the trees to conceal himself he scanned the bright flow and as his eyes adjusted to the sunlight saw four, no, he spotted a fifth—five nice fish. They were holding out in the middle, facing upcurrent to watch the foodlanes, their stream-lined bodies waving side to side in the moving water as they waited.

He stole downstream through the trees and as noiselessly as a cat stepping into cover where she senses a meal entered the current. Wading toward them in a crouch he flicked his fly onto the sliding brightness.

His pattern touched down delicately and floated, turning with the natural movements of the stream, toward the waiting trout. Tensed—thinking of nothing but fishing, his stare fixed on his pattern's pert pair of wings floating back downstream to him, he was smoothly gathering in his line in loops with his left hand.

One drifted up. Banking like a fighter plane peeling out of formation it turned to drift downstream following his fly, looking up at it, drifting with it.

Deciding it didn't like what it saw the fish made a swirl. Facing upstream again it swam effortlessly, with a few side-waves of its body, back upcurrent into its feeding slot among the others.

In the intensity of his excitement he laid his next cast out heavy. They didn't like this. They sidled, irritable in the water as his leader floated over them.

He stood still—made himself count to a hundred. Twice as he was counting one drifted up, riding the waterflow's vectors to the surface to sup, but he forced himself neither to skip a single number nor to hurry the count.

Crouching, commanding himself to relax, he laid his line upon the waters once more.

His Adams floated toward them and over them and on downstream of them without effect. They didn't give it a look. He tried again but it was the same. They cut it dead as it drifted over them, neither looking up at it nor moving in relation to it as it came toward them and passed over them.

Standing in the stream with his shoulders hunched in concentration and his chin lowered over his work, the hemlocks and pines towering above his bowed head, the current pressing against his legs and the morning sunlight pouring golden and warm down over the green Pennsylvania hills, he tied on eighteen inches of thinnest tippet and went down two fly sizes to a number twenty-two, the smallest he had.

He got everything ready, took a breath, and unfurled his cast.

The float was right. Two looked up. The larger of the two, moving its tail as it watched the fly pass overhead, drifted backwards downstream out of its feeding slot to drift along under the fly, eying it. Trimming its fins the trout glided up like a plane gaining altitude and fed. He struck hard. There was an explosion of spray in the sunlight and he was connected through his straining rod and humming line to the fish and through the fish to the stream and through the stream to the forest and the wide, living world.

Lifting his rod and stripping in line he pulled the zigzagging, thrashing little being downstream away from the others, so as not to spook them, and with his rod bobbing and dancing let the fish tire.

Spent, it permitted him to pull it toward him through the water and he bent down, wetting his hands, carefully held it, worried his fly free of the astounded, gaping jaws, held the slow-gulping little soul back under the water, and stroked its spine with a finger. In a flash it was a trout again and was gone.

Long afterward, talking of that day, he told me he had never in his life been more anxious to catch fish. He wanted to catch a hundred, a thousand, to hook and release it all away, all the vanity and the hounding and the lying . . .

The times were dangerous. Currents of power swirled out of control, forceful personalities swerving past each other without aim while the President, a decent man, stood at the center of things casting about weakly.

Hunter King was trying to restore order. He didn't talk much about Washington but when he did I was an avid listener. He liked me. I'm sure my obvious awe of him was the main reason—he was a terrific egotist. I don't mean to say that. It's not the whole truth.

I don't know what the whole truth is.

I want to try and see him for you, that first morning back out on his beloved stream after so many months . . .

The water flowing through the sunlit forest was idyllic and

the boy in him was filled with wonder to be here at the center of such beauty and movement and light. Part of him was innocence—a pink-healthy heart pulsing against the steel breast-plate of the man—and that part, the soul of the boy, was as capable of awe as his cruel part was corrupt.

After releasing that first fish I imagine him going after the rest in the pool with a cold eye, the same demons goading him on, there on our club's several miles of freestone water, as had driven him down all the power-corridors of his distinguished, difficult life.

He was short, five-seven with heavy, hulking shoulders and a pair of enormous forearms. He wasn't handsome but that face was impossible not to be impressed by—bulldog jut of chin, wide, adamant cheekbones, inquisitive eyes, forehead smooth like the brow of a Buddha, bald skull tight-skinned and glowing with health, dark-blotched permanently now from his thousands of days out-of-doors.

He fished the morning away with no sense of time or place. There was only the stream, its runs and slicks, its deep pools and splashing tresses of riffle-water, the play of the sunlight on the changing currents and all the bright trout under the water drifting up lazily to sip at his fly.

There's no sense of yourself, just the sun on your neck, the flowing water against your boots, your angelhair leader lying out across the currents in S-curves to your fly, floating downstream with your fly, your soul floating too with your fly's drift on the stream's moving face.

Lunch was a ham-and-cheese sandwich and a can of soda gulped in haste and he was back at it, crouched, intent, feeling with his booted feet for a steady stance on the bottom stones, wading upstream around boulders, stepping precariously, an arm out for balance, from rock to rock to cross above or below the deeper stretches, skulking through the trees to scout out where they might be lying in the transparent pools, calculating his approach, slipping down the bank to steal into the water, coming toward them in a crouch, his wreck of a hat pulled low over his dark glasses, fishing just as hard, down the waning hours of that afternoon, as he had done at the day's beginning.

It was getting toward evening. His seventy-year-old legs were tired. By morning they would be chalices of pain. The shadow cast by the forest lay out across the currents nearly to the far bank now. The heat had gone out of the day and as the sun rode down the sky toward the western mountains the light was going to that mellow gold that lingers, perhaps an hour, before June twilight.

He was hungry and knew he should go back but he kept fishing. Joan had stayed home as usual and he had no real obligation to get back to the clubhouse for dinner and so, that dilapidated hat yanked down over his bald head and his big, developed shoulders swinging side to side as he waded, he made his way on up the solitary evening stream.

He wanted to catch more and bigger fish—maybe it was just to get exercise—I don't know. I don't know what Hunter King wanted. I'm not sure he knew himself. He was not one to examine himself. Feeling was cut short by action. He had to be moving, had to have a project. I have seen him nap (it was like death—complete, motionless repose but for the appalling garglings emitting from his slack-jawed lips). But short of sleep he could not stand stillness. He wanted control, to mold all that he found around him, or else to anesthetize some old hurt—I don't know. He said he went further, that evening, than ever before. He went up the stream's north fork past the last pool we stock, into country the hunters among us cover come November but that to his knowledge had never been fished. The water was different this high up the mountainside. The stream narrowed down to, in some places, not more than fifteen feet across, pools above pools stepping away up the high hillside with smartly splashing waterfalls between, the water swift for this time of year, the late, weak sunlight, though stronger at this altitude than below, dying fast now and the air cool.

He took a few seven-inch natives from the difficult little pools and such fish are great sport in close cover like that but he was getting frustrated. Fishing from breakfast to dinner he hadn't caught anything over thirteen inches and he didn't think there'd be anything bigger this high but he wanted a good fish, one good fish. Night was coming. He had maybe an hour. To hike back down in total darkness would be dangerous and, stubbornly, knowing this, he pressed on, perching, scanning, casting, climbing, his open vest swinging like a prayer shawl as he toiled, his brow and neck sweaty now even with the evening cool coming on as he fished his way up—legs struggling, casts not always sharp—that hard slope.

He was well up the mountainside and out through the trees, if he turned, could glimpse the broad valley of farms and small villages stretching away in the soft light of the summer dusk. A slip of a breeze was moving through the forest. He turned his shirtcollar up. It was time to head back. The stream had grown steep and rocky, boulders, cliff-faces, sharp scarps of mountain-stone shadowing the water. It was late. Folks might worry, which, perversely, gave him pleasure. He was going on alone. The climb was practically impossible now, the way plunging into thick brush and branches that he had blindly to half-shut his eyes and crouchingly fend his way through as if struggling ahead into gale winds. Now suddenly the path became a path again and widened out into a stand of pines, the air cool and darkly sap-sweet here in the shadows of the trees, the carpet of needles giving with a soft springiness to his step as he walked through the pines' shadows to the grove's edge. He stepped from the trees out onto a ledge, a platform-like, narrow ridge of quartzite perhaps twenty feet above a black, still pool.

The forest was silent. No chainsaw growled at a distance. No faraway truck ground down through its gears, negotiating the grade of some distant expressway.

The stillness was so complete you could hear the timbrelly, ringing surf of the air's molecules against your inner ear.

He stood looking down at the water of the pool. He didn't think it had a trout in it but, looking down, thought he might as well try.

It would be his last pool. He would have to start down soon so as to get onto familiar paths before the light failed completely. There was a pebbly wash of a beach from which he would be able to cast. Making his way back through the gathering shadows of the pines and struggling down through the steep brush he came out beside the water.

He had room to side-and-roll-cast various patterns out over the impenetrable surface: a fat June bug plopped down, a bucktail streaked back and forth as if in distress, a pair of nymphs allowed to sink then handtwist-retrieved, jig-twitched, and tested with his favorite up-and-over, lolling, rolling motion.

But the pool was lifeless. The sun had been down half an hour. It was going to be cold this evening—good sleeping weather. Staring at the black face of the water, across which wisps of mist were beginning to steal, he gave a sigh.

He reeled in and hooked his fly to the ring for it on his rod.

He shouldn't've come, not this high, not this late. To do so had only dramatized his expectations so that having to start back now, empty-handed, was all the more disappointing. Turning from the water and pressing back through the trees and brush he was trying to remember which way he'd come.

There was a splash.

He froze, grinning. Turned in time to see, through the trees, the unmistakable concentric circles gentling out from where the fish had fed.

His head was down as he busied himself tying on a fair-sized elk-hair caddis, thinking to get his scissors out and clip the hackle off underneath so it wouldn't sit too high on the surface-tension—it hadn't sounded like a particularly big fish but at least it was a fish, here higher than he'd ever come—then back for a hot shower and food.

He waved some line out, pale green, double-tapered line shining faintly in the last shreds of light as it furled and unfurled in the air like the sign for infinity

then

waiting

an instant

his line out behind him in the dim

he flicked his rod forward stopping it

short

as if rapping his knuckles on a door

once.

In the split-second before his rod unloaded he was motion-less,

his line extended behind him

in the next frame of time—butt of rod the same, stopped, fisherman the same, motionless—willowy shaft bobbed forward

17

hurling line forward toward target-area in one fluid impulse, line unfurling toward where the rise had been and gently of a piece falling as exquisite, filmy leader and tippet leapt out over themselves exaltantly
    delicately
    his caddis
    alit
    without
    a ripple
"Take it," he whispered.

He gave his rod a twitch. His caddis hopped. Time un-spooled backward and came unraveled in that dusk light as he stood before the pool bent forward, peering into the gloam at his ghostly fly riding the scarcely-moving water.

The splash surprised him and he gave a start as the spray-shower went up. He raised his rod. It had hooked itself. Had it? Yes. It was on. It was on solid and it wasn't that bad of a fish either, shaking its head no-no-no in protest, splashing and slapping the water trying to dive—

He did not let it.

He coaxed some line in. It quit fighting a second. When he tried for more line the fish came alive again and was spanking and thrashing the water and he stood smiling at the situation. As it floated toward him and he smoothly stripped in line, bringing it to him, its gills opening and shutting, its tailfin slowly wagging, he marveled at it in his fatigue, and was satisfied.

Alive again without warning it shot away across the pool finning wildly. It raced back the other way across the surface like a speedboat planing—went under. The water was still. It made a spectacular leap, silvery, sleek body hanging, to his astonishment, on the very air before dropping back with a splash.

No sooner had it fallen back than it leaped again, clearing the water in a slashing trajectory more like a flying fish than a trout—it did this repeatedly, crossing the pool in a series of leaps. Puzzled, he kept his rod high and followed it, lowering his tip when it jumped. Now it sped off in a different direction, leaping clear, leaping clear—he'd never seen a hooked trout do this. With yet another surge it propelled itself higher still into the air, turning one crazed, horrified eye on the shadows beneath it—

The whole pool seemed to bulge.

The dark surface lifted, as if the fire-core of the planet itself were coming up. Bull-backed, shining gold, out of proportion to anything he had ever seen or heard or read about, muscling the water aside with a terrific swirl and lunging for his panic-stricken little trout's white belly the dooming jaws slammed shut.

The water began to lap, rhythmically, out against the sides of the pool.

Insolent—vast and menacing, it hung on the darkness. A brightness seemed to shine out around it, the great black spots and blotches covering its broad back glimmering and glowing and its tailfin, like a tall sail, not moving and the waves its coming had made riding out to the pool's edge to lap, like a miniature surf, against the gravelly beach where he stood staring at it.

It was holding an eleven-inch brook trout broadside in its jaws.

He stared at the silvery head of his little fish drooping—eye not dead but glassily dying—from the clamped-shut jaws.

After a time he came to himself and dreamily lifted his rod. As his line came taut the thing turned its head, his dead fish drooping from the shut jaws turning with the slow turning of the enormous head and slick, sullen eye.

It was looking at him.

He couldn't move.

Turning away, turning a shoulder to him, taking its time, seeming not to swim but rather, magically, to glide—drift—like a visual effect changing size on a screen, it carried its meal down out of sight stripping line from his reel in an arrogant series of clicks.

The tension on his line relaxed and when he lifted there was just the deadweight of the fish he'd caught. Deep, where the light does not reach, with a tailsweep the jaws ate their meal swimming at it and through it swallowing, the massive head wagging once, angrily, snapping his leader clean.

two

He came back that evening disheveled and contented, the line of white hair half-circling the base of his head damp with perspiration and matted from his hat, his strong-boned face aglow from the day's sun, his shirt and khakis unkempt.

He drank a beer and wolfed a plate of leftovers. We were his pale reflection. Eating greedily and sucking at his beer, his eyes shining with health (and his secret—a trout that would be a state record), he joked with us about fishing. He parried our questions about Washington. He listened to each of us, as we vied to say things to him. When he turned the beaconlight of his attention on you it was exhilarating. A faith in you you didn't have in yourself illuminated his eyes, and as he listened earnestly to what you had to say you knew it was all right, everything was all right. An almost palpable field of health and energy vibrated out around him, the work-roughened hands half-lifted, as he listened to you, as if to entreat you not to leave anything out about yourself—to tell him everything.

He yawned, slapped his belly, and trudged up to bed leaving us all feeling a little better.

He told no one (seeing the water heave like earth in the second after dynamite detonates, seeing the shoulder—black-spotted—turning, and the great jaws clamping shut with a slap not like thunder but like the lightning-shock-warp. He couldn't get the image out of his mind, eye—perfect black circle—lifeless as a frozen planet, and the great belly sagging from the carriage of the body, the whole structure too large, as if the design had been meant to fit something smaller, as if some absentminded god had created an elephant a thousand feet tall).

He went up to the pool the next day and got a drowned rat of a sculpin-imitation deep, but there was no action. He climbed down to water he knew. He fished for a few hours then turned, as if to climb again to the rock-walled pool, but didn't. He walked back to the clubhouse and ate lunch. After lunch, instead of heading back out into the sunlight he found himself walking up the noisy, uneven old stair and he fell into a dead sleep for the rest of the afternoon.

Hunter King's sense of humor shone out around his eyes. He loved all kinds of humor, just as he loved every kind of food, and when something struck him as particularly funny he would roar, giving himself up to a laughter he couldn't control, shaking, booming, tears streaming down his cheeks and his eyes twinkling at you conspiratorially. The joke was his and yours, the tearing, merry eyes seemed to say, on an unsuspecting world.

In conversation he would interrogate you with a perceptiveness that was uncanny. As the picture began to form for him he would lean forward, making shapes in the air with his hands, wanting always to be sure he was understanding exactly what you were trying to say. He would arrive at his picture of you and sit back, rubbing a work-scarred hand over his mind's protective cover. You didn't know it yet but your conversation with him was over. The beacon of his attention was ready to swing elsewhere. He'd finished piecing his picture together and was ready now to go on to something else. I'm not sure true understanding was of interest to Hunter King. I think he was threatened by the possibility something he couldn't control might be going on, and so, grilling you until he had an under-standing—however superficial—of you, he was getting his fix on you so as not to have to feel threatened. There might be subtleties, fine detail you wanted him to be aware of. He didn't want to know. He didn't want his snapshot complicated.

Yet he was so genuinely interested when he was interested, and his warmth was so warm when it was on, that in a kind of suspension—unable not to trust him—you stuck with him.

Hunter and Joan King's son, Peter, lives in New Zealand. He's a doctor. His sister Molly once told me that at dinner when they were growing up Hunter would light into the boy as if cross-examining a hostile witness, Hunter's face red—I have seen this—the war clouds tight, dark and low before the beetling brow, some great pain or anger driving him to attack, scarlet-faced, staring down at his plate hammering out the words, shaking the pain, twisting against it, chewing at it, hating it, unable to shake it, caught by it, wagging his head against it, unable to throw it.

I don't know what that deep anger was. I do know that his father, Sunderland King, described to me by people in a position to know as a tyrant at home, must surely have had some-thing to do with Hunter's really quite spectacular temper that you could see coming like spontaneous combustion, a bulging and reddening of the face, all pleasure and lightness going away and a heavy, dull, deadening, thunderous anger pounding in him out of all proportion to the moment.

Then, for a minute—many minutes, you wouldn't be able to reach him.

But if Hunter's father was responsible for the pain in Hunter, what then of Hunter's father's father? Might there not be some further pain, some further questions to be asked, there?

I don't know. There are always further pools, but it gets dark. You have to go back.

When I think about Hunter King I see him from so many angles he eludes me. I focus on a certain way he was and he moves out of the focus I've put him in because I realize, even as I'm seeing him, that he was also a different way. He moves off, drifts off—I change my way of thinking. I vary the angle of approach. He slides away, still there, neither out of reach nor in it. When I stop trying to understand him, in the corner of my eye he starts to rise into focus. The instant I look at him again he moves off, drifts off . . .

He went up to the rock-walled pool again that June week-end and this time he was ready to fish. It was hot. A stillness had descended over the mountains, an ugly, humid haze hold-ing forest and sky fast in a vice of damp pressure.

He stood there in the heat holding his rod and staring into the water in fascination, his eyes as expressionless as the pool, as if there were a voice coming from the water, or some eerie music stirring in it.

He swatted a cast out popping his fluorescent-orange inchworm down on the mirror-black. He didn't expect a response but wanted to try the surface before going under with nymphs and wets. With a smack a big minnow took. He gave a start and his heart accelerated—he had to smile at himself. He watched the silvery-dull baitfish floundering at the center of the pool.

He left it there awhile in its distress, to see if it would call something up.

In the gorse behind him an insect was making a tone like the buzz near a high-tension wire. With his free hand he got out his bandana and wiped the prickly sweat from his eyes. Around him, looming above him, the mountainside boulders and slabs seemed to vibrate in the density of the heat.

The little fish swam about disorientedly, pattering the water.

It looked small in the darkness. He stood watching it, the seconds going by in a windless flow. The little baitfish stopped struggling and he stared at it, floating, listless, atop the ton-heavy volume of water, a sardine-sized tarnished-silvery junkfish—he was staring at it—it hung there . . .

He cranked the minnow in, dragging it to him like a delinquent child yanked by the ear, and unhooked it and tossed it back and watched it disappear—the pool was as before.

He lifted his hat, his meaty fingers holding it by its tattered visor, to wipe his brow with the back of a hand.

He cut his leader back and tied on a bruiser of a crawdad and a large nymph without a name and hauled it all back, his line swinging more like a pendulum than a flowering flyline, and heaved it all out over the pool and watched it plop in and sink.

He waited.

—danced his flies surfaceward in the murk, giving them,

with a delicate juke, just that half inch's lift, that slight, startled jump away from the bottom that can convince a fish something nourishing is getting away.

Nothing happened.

He went to streamers. He fished a wet Royal Coachman, its ballroom-scarlet audacity enjoyable to look at. Working through his boxes he tried a Baron, a Candlestick Maker, a damselfly, an Akroyd, a Black Bomber, a Logie, a Rosborough Golden Stone, several sizes of muddler, a gnat and an ant and a scud.

The sun, which could not be seen, had gone lower behind the afternoon's gauze. The heat was not letting up. Tomorrow he would fly back. His first meeting was scheduled for after lunch and at that meeting he would be taking a set of important responsibilities away from a colleague, a man who had helped him, and he was trying to think how he might make it look like a promotion. It tired him to have to do this. It exhausted him to have to calculate—go cold and think—figure—how best to do what he knew, staring at the upside-down, motionless pines and huge boulders in the water, was necessary.

He was just sitting, not fishing. With the coming of twilight perhaps something would change. Maybe it would move. He sat watching the water. With evening's first cool maybe something would happen.

Evening was a long time coming in that dripping, static heat.

Watching the water he took his hat off to mop his brow. There was a strange chill. He half-rose, startled—it wasn't the air . . . the air was still . . . it wasn't anything. It was nothing, just the flat, lightless water. He sat again, slowly, not taking his eyes from where it lived.

Getting the tax bill the President wanted depended on making friends again with the Senate Minority Leader without giving in on the African ceasefire—also on whether or not he could outmaneuver the Treasury Secretary.

He thought about this.

Feeling in his pocket for his bandana he found it soaked so he unfolded it and spread it on a rock. He took out his spare and wiped his bald dome, forehead, cheeks, neck.

It hit him that the tax bill didn't matter. He allowed this thought to remain in his mind only because he was here, alone, in the wild. Flying back on the plane tomorrow he wouldn't believe it. Here, he could believe it. None of it, in the end, mattered. His youth came to him. The day's oppressive haze lifted and a breeze flowed over the mountainside. He remembered innocent summers, wandering with a rod for miles . . .

He put his hat on. Somewhere above was a star. Slowly, he reached for his rod.

He got back to work and the themes and rhymes of the cast, the holiness of angling, closed over him. He was not thinking of Washington or his youth or anything but the cast. On his third try he hooked something and lost it. On the next presentation he hooked it again and up through the shadows struggled a bright little trout of nine inches.

Releasing it, he thought he'd better wait. He didn't want to disturb the pool catching little ones. If the little ones were still active it probably meant the thing hadn't come out of its lair yet.

He sat down. It was nearly dark. Now in the ghostly twilight the tree toads began. Their singing sounded like thousands of tiny silvery bells shaken in thousands of infinitesimal silvery tumblers.

With a thrill he realized he could stay here. He realized, with mounting excitement, that it was what he wanted to do. He remembered no mention of rain and the negatives—he was supposed to call Joan—back at the Club they would worry—he had a plane to catch in the morning—only made the prospect more exciting. He felt an almost unbearable glow of well-being to be here deep in the forest and high up the mountainside, alone in the summer night.

Over the decades he'd been out in tents and under lean-tos but not this, not to sleep in the open under a nighttime sky, since boyhood.

He stood and feeling his way to the water's edge in the darkness fished his wet flies deep—there was pressure and when he hauled on his rod he felt something heavy against him and he tried to get an angle and some leverage on the force moving evenly away from him in the night, but his line went slack.

During the minutes it took him to calm down he read his pulse first at one-ten, then, as he began to relax, at eighty. Fumbling his pocket-flash out he fixed his leader, got two more flies tied on, and cast many times and—feeling his way clumsily in the night—from various angles. He moved tentatively, excited, hearing his big flies drop in when he blindly cast them and blindly, tingling in the blackness, waited, rod in hand, line running into the night . . . but nothing happened. He quit at last and rested, breathing, his heart going, the night black before his eyes.

The sense of the forest's million trees was overwhelming. Like an unclean wind a depression such as he had never experienced swept him. It was a sense not of unreality but of life as a dull-glimmering struggle without purpose. He saw life as a shadow. Tears of fear bulged. Fumbling in the blackness he pulled his boots and vest off. He half-sat half-slid onto the stones and sitting back, resting back against a pillow of tough thick grass, gritted his teeth. The night seemed to deepen around him as he sat there, teeth clenched, waiting for it to pass.

Now and then something went by, a rustling and stirring in the unseen woods, and this comforted him. He didn't like snakes but was afraid of no other animal and to hear possums, skunks—a bear perhaps, moving about made him feel better.

The darkness was alive. The years parted to reveal, in his memory, the time he had climbed out of bed, too terrified of the dark to bear it any longer, and trundled down the long hallway to his parents' room.

His father had walked him back down the hall to his room tucking him in and sitting down on the edge of his bed. To help him with his fear of the dark his father told him to concentrate on all the wonderful things going on out in the night on the other side of the windowscreen: porcupines waddling and poking about, owls cruising past the stars, night flowers opening and glint-eyed raccoons carrying their supper down to the stream's currents to wash it.

It had made him feel better then and it did now. Perhaps he was just exhausted. Turning on his side and getting his head comfortable against the pillow of grasses he snuggled for sleep, which—he didn't expect it—hit him like a bass slapping a worm.

Somewhere in the night he woke. He rubbed his eyes. There were stars, oceans of them, an infinity of them flung across the sky. He wept in gratitude. A sky filled with stars—to wake, here, under it—swelled his heart out beyond itself into a pacific enormity of stillness somehow like where the stars themselves hung, coldly shining.

He told himself for God's sake to stop crying. Get control. This caused him, as he lay gazing up, to feel what he was seeing as so truly wondrous that he burst out bawling like a baby. Nothing like this had ever happened to him. He told himself to stop. Suddenly he wasn't crying; he was laughing. Here on a mountaintop in the small hours of the morning shouting with laughter he was. It was extraordinary. It was ridiculous. The darkness had fallen quiet all around him, a thousand large and little eyes and cocked heads wondering, in the night, what new kind of beast this could be.

In a while he got up and made a few casts without result. Lay down again. Slept. Then he was awake. It was still perfectly dark but something was different. There was an expectancy, a tension on the night. The minutes slid by gradually and a faint, colorless light crept around the edge of the world. The light grew, making visible the shadows of the great rocks. Nothing had color. All was gray—shadow and silhouette—but it was the world, and it was beginning to take form.

A bird twittered in the shadowlight.

The trees were green now and the sky—stars disappearing—eggshell blue. More than one bird was singing and the forest had begun to stir, the light growing, the forest coming clear in its slightest detail.

Kneeling at the edge of the pool he splashed black water into his face with cupped hands. He got his gear sorted out and tried a few casts. Looking at his watch as the sun appeared atop the ancient mountains, starting to think of what he had to say to the people he would be meeting today, he set off down the mountainside.

He enjoyed our consternation thoroughly. Around midnight groups had set out in jeeps, but no one had thought to go up along the north fork. When the wire services picked it up and it received a touch of play over the next few days he was delighted. The whole episode delighted him enormously. He'd slept out under the stars and worried everyone and although he tried to pretend otherwise you could see the whole thing gave him the greatest pleasure.

three

Marian called to me and waved. She'd brought her sketch pad along and was sitting cross-legged in the sunlight working on a birch while Richard practiced his clapping. Sean, our firstborn, was not interested and had wandered off.

I walked along the stream scouting the water. Now I was looking at a bright, rippleless pool with fish in it. Kneeling in the grasses I watched them, trying to memorize their positions. Walking downstream I stole into the cool flow and taking one slow, deliberate step at a time waded back upstream toward where I'd seen them.

I couldn't see them. The light shone wrong. As I slowly, smoothly edged through the water I was trying to get a sense of where I had knelt in the meadowgrass when I'd spotted them.

I took one more punctilious, slow step and there they were,

fat, silvery arrows in the brightness, shadowy heads and shining, tapering bodies finning easily as they held in their feeding positions watching for food.

As I watched one fed, leisurely, and nosed back down. I lifted my rod to cast and there were trout everywhere scattering, fleeing, running into each other finning wildly, zigzagging, crisscrossing, diving under rocks, scooting under banks—a fat one shot downcurrent passing within a foot of my leg wriggling like a berserk firework and the stream was empty.

Quietly, the water flowed as before.

They are that skittish; a rod or even your line waving in the air, even fifty feet from them through the stream-ceiling they look up through, can spook them completely.

I splashed shoreward and climbed out dripping. Marian was working at her sketch, keeping part of an eye on Richard.

Watching my wife as she worked, her plain, honest features dark with concentration as, a hand on Richard, she made quick strokes with her pencil, I realized how lucky I am.

My anger went down and I stood looking out across the meadow, half a mile of open countryside that we fish by agreement with the farmer who owns the land and pastures his cattle there. In the distance, out over the grassy plain, his herd of occasionally groaning cows was plodding along, and further to the south the foothills of the deep-green Pennsylvania mountain were his cornfields, luxuriant now in their final month, with black crows flapping back and forth against the blue.

I stood there taking it all in, the warm August air moving against my face.

I wasn't much of a fisherman but it was a nice day and a nice place to be and my anger at my own stupidity was gone and I was ready to get into the stream and try again. Walking through the waist-high grasses, paying attention to where I was stepping where the cows had been, I followed the water.

In the next run there were trout. One fed—quick bulge of current, telltale circle disappearing. I wondered what it's like to hold yourself against the flow's push. Insects and beetles drifting downstream on the surface light must seem like planes flying low overhead, steadily approaching. Nymphs tumbling and turning over the streambottom stones must rush out of the waterblur at you like space-movie fighters wheeling and tumbling suddenly out of the blackness of deep space.

Drifting a weighted nymph over the bottom I picked up a lovely little brown. The first fish of the day always pumps me up and when I'd released him I hurried to get my nymph back down under. The cast didn't come down right and I annoyedly started a roll-pickup to cancel my mistake and turn it into a proper cast when something odd happened and my line was taut and my rod bent with a terrific pressure and the fish of my life took off upstream with a whizzing, high-pitched shriek of reel.

From the bank came an excited shout. I turned.

Hunter King, fists on hips—elbows out—legs apart, stood like a grinning capitaz of stevedores, assessing the situation.

The monster muscled upstream making my reel sing and when I tried to thumb it to slow him I just hurt my thumb. Hunter was shouting turn it, get it off balance.

I shouted over my shoulder at him that that was what I was trying to do.

Marian's voice called out—she'd come to see what all the shouting was about.

Not turning my head I shouted that I'd caught a very big one.

"Good!" she cried.

I turned a second to glance at her.

She was holding Sean, whom fishing did not interest, by the hand and hefting Richard in her other arm. Richard's pudgy features were dazed under the ruffles of his white sunbonnet. He looked out over his mother's arm at nothing, or at what only cats and infants can see, a fat arm hanging listless on the air, as a senile prelate might in his oblivion bless, from his balcony, a piazza without any people in it.

Turn him Hunter was shouting, turn him, get him off balance. Stretching upstream to where the monster had stopped and was sulking, way up in the headwaters of the run, my line was out at least a hundred feet.

I did turn him. He gave a little and I got some line back.

Keep the pressure on Hunter shouted, don't let him rest.

I shouted over my shoulder that I was doing fine.

The fish made a run, trying to get in under the bank where the current had hollowed out a den. Because he was moving I was able to get some purchase on him and turn his head from the direction in which he wanted to go, and I had him sideways to the current too now so that he was deprived of the strength of the current—couldn't add it to his own, and I drew him toward me, gaining line, with Hunter shouting instructions, and I was pulling him, unable to see him where he fought me in the murk, when with a stupendous surge, whizzing line off my reel, he swam in under the bank.

Hunter came jogging through the grasses with a big stick. Getting down practically on his face he reached in under the cutbank to poke, trying to scare the fish back out.

This annoyed me, as it was my trout.

It worked—he chased it into the current again shouting here

it comes here it comes keep your line taut!

At last I could sense it tiring. Suddenly it offered no resistance, floated right up, drifted to my side.

I stared at it.

It was twelve inches long. I had thought I was onto a devil or an angel but it was just a fish, and not a very impressive one. I'd foul-hooked a normal-sized trout just forward of its tailfin: all that mysterious pulling power had been nothing more than leverage.

The arctic-blue eyes rose to meet mine. He had a way of lowering his head like a bull and lifting his eyes to stare at you from under the great bone-ledge of his brow.

He was laughing.

He roared, rubbing his eyes, shaking his head. He quieted down a moment but the laughter was all through him and he couldn't help himself. He threw his head back and roared.

He was in a fight for his political life. The Treasury Secretary, a ruthless infighter, had embarked on a methodical, clever campaign certain to end with one or the other of them out of government.

It was a tense, trying time for him. As ambitious at seventy as he'd been at thirty he simply could not stand the thought of losing. His ability to be self-deprecatory, over a hand of cards say, was not humility. It was a form of release from a need to win so obsessive he knew it would turn on him and consume him if he did not from time to time free himself from it.

I've done some digging into his early years, and the silver trophies are there—the blue ribbons are there, and later on the honorary degrees and chairmanships—he couldn't stop. He couldn't stop needing to win. If he made a mistake at cards he would mock himself (before anyone else could) succinctly. But if you tried to tease him about it the ice-blue eyes would change. He would nod, with scarcely a smile, as if to say yes, inadvertently I did something amusing and we've laughed about it now that's enough.

Done laughing at me he slapped his knees, refreshed. He was up, ready for action. He greeted Marian as deferentially as if she had borne him, here beside the sun-glinting waters, gifts far in excess of anything he actually deserved.

The boys he acknowledged with a neutral smile. They were of an age neither to be competed against nor learned from. Richard had come out of his fresh-air stupor and appeared to be practicing crying expressions. Moods played across the chubby face like sunlight and rain squalls playing across open country-side on a March day. He would smile beautifully and then, surprised as a handful of neurons fired, grimace and screw up his plastic little features as if to howl.

Marian was hefting and jiggling the sunbonneted mandarin in her arms to try and postpone the inevitable. Hunter turned to me with a rueful smile. The magnificent salt-and-pepper brows were knitted in concern, now that he'd laughed his soul clean at my expense, that I not feel too bad about it all. He came to my side and threw an arm over my shoulder. In conspiratorial tones he told me about the time he'd caught a truck tire instead of a salmon. I was laughing. He was laughing. I was laughing more than I wanted to be.

Those glittering wells of eyes, the physical fact of him looming over you, his energy, his magnetism—his enthusiasm when he turned his charm on . . . I see I've written "loomed," and so it seems in my memory, though he was shorter than I am by several inches.

He put his hands on his hips.

Looking at a point in the air somewhere around the level of my knees he said: "Well. You'd better come have lunch with us."

The possibility of a rejection seemed to unnerve him.

"Molly's up," he said. "I'm meeting her up at the shelter. We're driving to a wonderful little spring we know. We've ten times the food we need."

Talking about him that evening in our room, Marian, with my feet in her lap, massaging them as I stroked her moving forearm, said wasn't it interesting how he'd put his invitation: "You'd *better* come have lunch."

"He meant it politely."

"I know," she said.

I moved her bracelet around on her wrist as she rubbed my feet.

She'd taken the boys back. Sean had been bored and it could have been pleasant to take Richard up the mountain only if a supply-entourage of kitchens, diaper-changing units, toy quartermasters and crib engineers could've followed in train, so she had begged off. And this seemed very all right with Hunter, who—I almost missed it—nodded with quick approval when she told me to go on without her.

I kissed her goodbye and told the boys I'd see them later. Sean was examining the fabric of his mother's shorts and Richard, about finished practicing, seemed ready now to begin bawling in earnest. Hunter and I trudged across the meadow to where he'd parked his jeep and we got in and he got it started and we bumped into the shadows of the forest on the old road and wound along the creek for a bit then turned off on the more rutted, rocky trail-road that shortcuts up to the shelter.

I was pretty excited. The hand on the wheel had shaken the hands of prime ministers and monarchs. We rode in silence because he was silent. He had that air, the starch of command. It made you want to chatter but I didn't. I wouldn't've dared, his silence was so definitive as he drove casually watching the rutty road as it tilted out of the forest at us.

Molly King sat at the weathered table under the shelter's split-log roof with her feet flat on the bench, her knees under her chin, her arms wrapped around her legs and her gaze directed out over the water.

Her back was to us. Her fishing cap was pushed back on her head and her hair fell not quite to her shoulders, thick, girlish hair filled with blond and brown tones and streaked gray, not quite combed and a little wild-looking, as if she'd been swimming and were letting it dry untoweled.

She turned toward us as her father's jeep engine approached and the look on her face wasn't girlish. She was staring at us with a strange, neutral expression.

Hunter cut his speed with an abrupt downshift that riding the clutch he tried to make graceful and we slid with a gravelly crunch to a stop.

He leaned forward, his arms folded over the wheel, looking past me at her.

"Hi Daddy."

Her sensual, thin lips were crooked, a sort of smirky smile that when you looked at it a second time you realized wasn't. The eyes were stone gray. She was looking at me and the forest sounds and the play of the light down through the trees went away into those steady, gray eyes.

"You've met Joe," he informed her. "He's having lunch with us."

I said I would get in back. I was half out of the jeep with a foot on the metal step and a leg dangling but she lowered her eyes and said don't bother. Putting a hand against my back she bent me forward to make room and squeezed behind me and was in.

Hunter muscled it into first, clutch in.

"Do any good?"

"Well," she said. "I got seven. Is that good?"

"That's good Moll."

"Good," she said with—it seemed to me—a sliver of a real smile.

I said nothing. I could see her in the rearview mirror.

Grasping the wheel with both hands he turned to look at her.

"Any nice ones?"

She pulled her hat off. Making a claw of her hand she raked her nails through her hair.

"One nice one," she said.

He spun the wheel and we bumped back onto the trail-road.

"How big?"

"Fifteen inches."

"That's a good fish Molly."

"It was."

"Did he put up a battle?"

"Yep."

She uttered the word with a hiccup-intake of breath, as if some pain had twinged her.

He waited, lifting his chin to glance at her in the rearview as we bumped along, but apparently she had nothing more to say.

She sat with a grace that was all the more impressive because she seemed unaware of it—right knee lifted, right foot braced, arm draped over knee, long, slender fingers dangling casually, as if a fashion photographer had arranged her.

I was looking at her in the rearview as we heaved and rattled up the mountainside through the forest.

She wore a shirt of forest-dark green under her fishing vest, and the orange kerchief she wore tied around her tall neck was perfect, daring—too much on another woman . . .

Marian stopped massaging at this point to ask if I had a crush on Molly King. I wisely admitted that I did but said it was no reason not to give me my foot massage. She said it was a reason to tickle my feet, and did so.

Leafy branches rushed at us, slapping the windshield and scratching the jeep's sides as we lurched up the old trail-road.

Molly let her slender frame be swayed as the jeep's undercarriage took the ruts. The dun-gray eyes gave nothing away. She let the motions of the ride sway her—head lolling when the jeep's wheels hit a rock—it was enormously attractive. I was watching her. I think she knew it. We took a jolt and apparently deciding he was going too fast Hunter slowed, straightening his arms. He gripped the wheel at ten and two o'clock and leaned back, erect, to drive looking straight ahead.

We rode awhile that way, the musculature of his forearms prominent above the jiggling wheel, the weather-chapped lips a ruled horizontal line.

Something occurred to him. Half turning his head he asked me in a stage whisper if we should tell Molly about our trout.

I smiled.

"Well," he began, settling into his seat, and the story, like a puppy circling to lie down, "I was wandering around down in the meadow when I happened on our friend Joe here fighting what had to be the biggest fish ever caught. I mean to tell you, the biggest trout ever caught, from the way his rod was bent . . ."

He laid it on, building suspense, describing my trembling line, the runs of my "enormous" trout, me in the water, himself on the bank—then devilishly he fell silent. Forcing a laugh I had no choice but to take the burden of making fun of me on myself. I couldn't very well say nothing. Cleverly and with obvious pleasure he had manipulated me into a position of having to describe the embarrassing scene myself. I know I'm too sensitive but it was frustrating how even in the littlest matters he was forever, instinctively—unconsciously I think, calculating and positioning.

I explained that the fish had been foul-hooked.

Molly didn't laugh.

She leaned forward.

"Doesn't one," she asked, "often foul-hook walleye?"

Marian thought this brilliant. It diffused any embarrassment to me by redirecting the conversation without changing the subject. Hunter watched the road. His daughter had mock-innocently put him down without being in the least impolite. She had done it effortlessly, like—without thinking—moving the correct chess piece to block, by simply refusing to get his joke. Now if he explained that the point was not that one foul-hooks walleye but that Joe here had spent half an hour thinking he was onto the fish of the decade, he—Hunter—would be in the position of having to reexplain a joke to someone who hadn't found it funny the first time.

Marian smiled at the thought as she stroked, stroked, the curve of my flatfooted instep.

"Well," Hunter snapped in the voice of a chairman whose

board has strayed, "*so*. Did your fifteen-inch fish—" impatient glance in the rearview "—take on the surface?"

"Under the water."

"On a wet?"

"A dry," she said seemingly thinking of something else.

He waited.

"It got wet and sank," she said. "I fished it that way."

"Good girl."

She threw an elbow up to protect herself but was only, I realized, taking her vest off. Wriggling free of it she folded it, checking to make sure the pockets were shut, and laid it on her lap as we bumped along. She folded her hands on it.

Her grace was remote, like that of a ballerina performing in solitude, thinking something through, alone, with her body.

Her face was small-looking in the dark little rearview and even when I wasn't flicking my eyes to the jiggling mirror to glimpse her, I was thinking about her.

Their favorite luncheon spot was a spring, a pile of boulders set back in the shadows of the forest—water pure as truth and stinging cold purling from the mouth of a lichened, encrusted pipe.

We brought the coolers from the jeep and balanced them on the backs of the rocks and stood looking down through the trees to where the stream, far below, was giving off winks of sunlight as it flowed.

It was cooler here in the shadows where the black boulders crowded in a tumble. Kneeling and twisting my neck to drink of the icy trickle I could feel the cool of the shadows of the trees on me and feel, against my skin, the damp of the barely perceptible mist that hung on the air. The cold, delicious water spilled from the rocks and I drank. I could hear the sounds of the forest, birds singing, the droning and sawing of insects as I shut my eyes and twisting my neck with puckered lips sipped.

Molly had taken her neckerchief off. Unbuttoning the top buttons of her shirt she lay back into a patch of sunlight. She folded her arms behind her head, shutting her eyes.

I looked at her.

Hunter was unpacking the coolers.

I couldn't decide whether I thought she was homely, with those strange, thin lips, or exotic. From a certain angle she almost struck you as odd-looking, but she wasn't. She was unusually beautiful. I looked down at her. She lay on her back, the fabric of her shirt drawn tight over her champagne-glass breasts the way she had her arms folded behind her head. The effect fascinated me. She was close to forty-five yet as I looked at her, the muscles of her face utterly relaxed, eyes shut, lids not fluttering, her expression as calm as a breezeless sea, she seemed not to have an age. She could have been twenty. Or sixty.

I wondered what went on inside her, if she had secret thoughts—I was looking at her only a few seconds then I came to myself and was embarrassed and I turned quickly away trying to appear not to be doing so. I tried to help Hunter with unpacking the coolers but it was his show. I felt as if I would put my hand on the wrong jar or unwrap something he wanted to keep covered, so, as if he'd elbowed me, I stood to one side not knowing what to do as he finished elaborately laying out on the rocks the extensive luncheon he'd had prepared.

"Moll?"

She stirred. An eye opened. "Hm?"

"Joseph?"

"Yessir?"

"Ready for some lunch?"

"Okay," she said drowsily.

"Sure," I said.

She sat up, blinking, to receive a chicken-salad sandwich and a frosted can of beer.

As I began to eat I realized how hungry I was.

"This is good," she chewed.

"It is," I agreed.

"It is," Hunter munched.

With his sleeves rolled up and the farmer's forearms— elbows out—making the legs of a right triangle below his dripping sandwich as he lifted it to his teeth, he turned his head to the side and ripped into his food.

"It's beautiful here," she said.

He stopped in mid-bite. The look he flashed her was one of pure pleasure in the knowledge that she was enjoying herself.

She ate her sandwich, her face partly hidden by her hair, and he was watching, satisfied.

He returned to his sandwich.

"I'm glad you like it," he chewed.

"How much land," she asked as she took a bite, "does the Club own?"

"How much land have we got now Joe?"

He tossed the question at me out of the side of his mouth as he tore, with bulging eyes, into what was left of his sandwich.

He knew better than I did how much land we have but he wanted to see if I knew.

"You know better than I do sir," I said. "I think it's twenty-seven-hundred acres isn't it?"

"Almost right," he nodded tearing an uncooperative piece of ham in two with a sideways, savage wag of his head. "Twenty-eight-hundred as a matter of fact. We got Old Man Buchanan to buy up that little farm over on the other side of West Mountain."

"That's a lot of real estate," she said.

There it was, the faintest irony, a barely perceptible whet-edge on her voice when she spoke to him.

"When was it you were last up Moll?"

"Last September."

"That's right," he said wiping his lips. "We brought the McCalls along didn't we."

"Yep."

The sun slid behind a cloud and all the light in the forest went out. Spots that weren't there danced before my eyes.

I held my sandwich.

"How are they?"

"The McCalls?"

"It's been too long since I've seen 'em."

"Well," she said, "they're fine."

She threw her head back finishing her beer. Lowering her emptied can to a knee she swallowed. She seemed to think of something.

She spoke now in a heavy, almost weary voice, looking neither at her father nor at me.

She said: "Mother's fine."

He hadn't asked. He hadn't mentioned Joan. Then I realized that that was her point. She sat looking down at her beer can, pressing her thumbs against its middle. Hunter's big fingers closed over a fly that had tumbled from his fishing vest's fleecy breast-patch onto the khaki of his trousers. His chin touching his chest, he lifted the tiny fly back up to the breast-patch to relodge it there.

"Well," he said to himself. "That's fine."

Molly bent the can one way then back the first way, worrying the metal, heating the molecules along the crimp until with a click it came apart.

I made myself take bites of sandwich. The silence between them was very loud.

The cloud had been a small one and as it blew off the face of the sun the forest came alive with light, the three of us, perched on the rocks, no longer shadows.

Hunter King spoke his daughter's name.

She didn't answer. She was toying with fitting the two pieces of her can back together along the jagged tear. She fiddled with the metal halves casually, as if only partially interested in fitting them together. Her hair fell forward.

He spoke her name a second time. It came in a whisper. I made a great, intricate project of my sandwich.

Hunter and his daughter started to talk at the same time and she stopped and he kept on, his desperation jutting like a fracture through his attempt to keep his voice steady.

"I want you to understand," he was saying, "I want to explain it to you so you'll understand it. Your mother and I. All the . . . the time I've—traveling I've—" He stopped, his hands fallen open, palms up, like cracked eggshell halves. He sat looking at his hands. "I guess," he said. "Sometimes two people . . ."

Again he stopped, as defenseless as I've ever seen him. Molly got to her feet and began packing away the picnic things and he sat there staring at her, his need alighting without impact on the unreadable, smooth surface of her calm.

Listening as I described the scene Marian lifted my feet from her lap and set them on the glossy cheap paint of the clubhouse bedroom floor. She sat in thought, tapping a finger as I talked.

Hunter slapped his knees.

"*Well*," he said into the ringing silence in which Molly moved about packing up, "are we ready?"

Swallowing I tried to say "Sure." I coughed some sandwich out. I scrambled to my feet to see if I could help her. She shook her head, working deftly.

"I thought we'd drive down to the river," he said glancing about with trapped eyes for something to pack.

I said I'd promised Marian I'd check back in with her.

He drew back, looking me over as if trying to determine how I could possibly want to do anything other than be with him and his daughter.

He turned away. He said they would drop me at the Club.

I picked a cooler up.

"Wait," he was telling her, "let me give you something."

He had his fly boxes out.

"Here."

She took from him the hoary, caddis-like hopper he proffered.

"Try it on a dead drift under the film," he told her, peering into his box to rummage for more, "like when you caught that fifteen-incher this morning. Oh and here—"

We waited as he poked about trying to find what he was looking for, then he had it and—pleased with himself—was holding it out to her.

"Here. A little inchworm. No one ties these anymore. Not this way anyway. And here's a backup one."

She took the flies from him.

"That's plenty," she said.

"There's one other."

"Really."

"I want to give you this one little other one. If I can just find it."

"I'm fine Dad."

"They're all mixed up. It's here somewhere."

I stood holding the cooler.

He stood on the big rock picking among his flies in their slots and trays and compartments, lost in what he was doing.

"Dad."

"Just a second."

"I don't want any more."

"Here. See? See the egg sac? See how I use pink for that?"

"I don't want them."

He took her hand, placed the flies on her palm, and closed her fist over them.

She looked at her shut fist.

"I don't want them," she said.

"I don't need them Molly. It's nothing. I've got more than I could possibly ever use."

"It's not nothing!"

I stared at her.

Taking a step back, astonished, as if she'd struck him, he was too nonplussed to take the flies back from her as she stood angrily holding them out.

Turning fast like a fish swirling she cast the bright little patterns down in a scatter on the rocks.

"It's not nothing," she said in a low voice.

She stood rigid.

"It's all right," he said taking a step.

But it wasn't.

He stood there. I stood there wishing I could be someplace else. She was hunkering down and searching over the mossy, damp rocks to pick up what she'd thrown down.

I asked if I could help.

She shook her head curtly.

Going forward on her knees and propping herself with a hand, the unbrushed, gray-gold hair swinging forward, she got the last one.

She got to her feet.

Her father took a step toward her, unable to meet her eyes, and he was reaching out to take his flies when with a toss of the head she turned and dropped them in her shirtpocket and buttoned it and was bending down to fit the plastic top back on the second cooler and latch the latch.

Marian tapped her finger. She leaned forward, picking my feet up and returning them to her lap. She sat stroking my flat insteps as we talked. I said it had been as if I weren't there, or were their employee. I was supposed to keep my eyes lowered and my ears shut as my superiors quarreled. Or perhaps they assumed they were so fascinating I—anyone—would consider it a privilege mutely to attend their argument.

Marian nodded.

"People like that," she said, "are like that."

My dad's family would sooner fly to a different continent than argue. Marian's folks quarrel and weep as naturally as they breathe. But I had never encountered such a quick, truncated drama of simultaneously flaunted and repressed passion as Molly and her father unleashed and shut off there among the black boulders by the spring.

I can see her, tall in her long-visored hat, turning to carry a cooler away down through the trees. I can see the gray-gold hair tumbling from under the back of her cap as she steps, carrying the cooler by its handles, carefully over the roots and fallen branches of the forest floor.

He put his hands on his hips. He looked down, the big jaw set. He murmured, not looking at me, that they would drop me at the Club. He walked away through the sunlit woods, the bearish back with the yellow plaid of his shirt stretched tight across it turning, wearily, side to side as he went.

I followed.

I guess when you come from generations of builders and wielders of power you learn to be efficient in your quarrels. Your passion stays reined in because you know you will need that energy and have learned not to lavish it. When it comes out you cut it off. You put the lid back on and latch the latch.

He had worked hard, serving three presidents with distinction. During the years in between he had lived—in theory—in the old house of porches and chimneys and awnings set back in a grove of hickories atop a green expanse of lawn along a street of such houses, trees, and lawns in that northern Pennsylvania river town.

But in reality he had lived in planes. He had lived in hotel suites and boardrooms from London to San Francisco. He insisted on overseeing the family's affairs personally. He joined every board of trustees and regents that asked him. He attended seminars, conferences, conventions. Success didn't come easily to him. No coups, no brilliant strokes, grace Hunter King's record. He was a bull, a plodder and a rammer, sly perhaps but never brilliant. He had to work hard to accomplish all he accomplished. Why then, when he could have been a gentleman-sportsman and passed his days wading the sparkling currents (which I suspect was the life a great part of him yearned for) did he choose to live as he did?

I don't know. Maybe tradition demanded it. Maybe his

child's rage against the father drove him forth into a world of struggle. From what people who knew Sunderland have told me it's possible. But if Sunderland King was the drawn-shades ogre everyone says, how do you explain his walking Hunter back down the hallway and tucking the boy in and sitting on the edge of the bed to tell him, against his fear of the dark, to think of all the wonderful things going on out in the night on the other side of the windowscreen? That doesn't sound like a tyrant to me, and it was Hunter himself who told me that story.

It doesn't add up. It never does. It can't be made neat. For a long time I wanted to tie everything up so I could understand it, but it isn't possible. It's a blur, pouring at you, never one way. Through the curtaining border separating your unconscious from the sun-filled still of your daylight mind tumbles such a melee of debris that to think it could ever be organized and categorized and understood is to set yourself up, believe me, for pain.

four

Marian's a lawyer. If you ask her a question she says things like: "That's two questions." With her Heidi face and auburn hair that she likes to wear up in a loose chignon, or braids, she can look like a Central European peasant. She has a good, linear mind and will think a thing through, that finger tapping, to a conclusion highly likely to prove correct. I respect her judgment. Her mind isn't complicated. I think her brain cells are lined up all pointing in the same direction. She can concentrate on a thing and stay on it, thinking, until she reaches her conclusion about it. I can't do that. I have a good mind too but I think it's a mind of a different kind. I see a thing one way then almost at once I see it differently then I'll see it the first way again, or a third way. I get little bouts of dyslexia when I'm reading—writing . . . I think various sections of my brain cells must be aimed in different directions—I don't know. I can see the world opposite ways at once, which is probably why I'm neat. Marian, who sees the world simply, is messy—not sloppy, just not neat, her desk a clutter, clothes on the floor, Richie's toys underfoot, that kind of thing. She doesn't need to be neat.

I don't always necessarily know it when she's thinking something through. She doesn't always sit tapping her finger. Moving a lawn sprinkler, passing me a trash bag, holding Richard while I fish, trailing a hand down me on a night we won't be making love, opening a Christmas present or doing her aerobics on the living-room rug, she will be thinking something through, something important to her, something about us, the boys, an upcoming deposition . . . then out of the blue and without preface she'll say what's on her mind.

"She intrigues you," she stated after a long silence as we drove home that August weekend with Richard and Sean asleep in the back.

I made the mistake of asking what she was talking about and she stared at the lifeless miles of highway until I said: "You mean Molly King?"

She watched the road. That was what she meant.

It was true. I was drawn. Nothing would come of it but I was fascinated—what did I think I was doing? I don't know. There was a cool, a remoteness, before which I was as helpless as the art lover circling back again and again through the gallery to stand before the same wordless, velvet-dark portrait.

I knew little about Molly King. She was well-read. Knew the courtly sports, had never married, worked—to occupy herself—teaching French and Spanish down at Bucknell. Yes. I was intrigued. I was attracted. When she had unbuttoned the top buttons of her shirt to lie back in the sunlight and fold her arms behind her head, shutting her eyes, it had seemed not that she was unconscious of her allure but that she assumed the world would know it was to look but not touch.

I had followed her gestures and movements with a fascination partly instinctive, drifting alongside her in the sun-shadowy flow of the minutes, wanting to touch.

"A little," I said.

Marian said nothing. I drove, leaving it alone.

We'd been married eight years. Before Marian I'd been living a life of circles, putting in long hours at the City Desk at the paper where I work then long hours at home writing the little essays and stories that I kept polishing and dismantling. I would get up from my typewriter and work on the 1870 townhouse I'd bought, sandpapering, caulking, drywalling—then go back to the writing area I'd set up to pretend I was Crane or London until it started going nowhere again. I would go out and have a beer with friends, fall asleep, go to work, go home and write, go west and fish, meet a woman, part, sandpaper, wire, stain, spackle, hammer, revise, delete, fall asleep and get up and go in to the paper. It was winding around itself, piling up, to no result. Then at some friends' I met Marian and I was history. I guess she was too. Well, I know she was. We've been lucky. I have never in my life met anyone so utterly without guile as my wife. Most of us put on a face. We make myths up about ourselves, lie a little—to the world, to ourselves—about ourselves. It's all right, I'm not criticizing it, we're just naturally protecting ourselves. But not Marian. She faces life with a sincerity, an utter inability to dissemble, that I sometimes find exceedingly disconcerting and most certainly could not live without.

After my lunch that afternoon with Molly and Hunter at

the spring, when I checked back in at the Club Marian kindly shooed me back out on the stream. I decided to go down to the river. It's hard fishing and I don't go there often but that afternoon for some reason I did. Rippleless and swift, the main current too deep to wade, the flow pours silently over great submerged boulders, the water a dark brown, not a splash, not a gurgle as the current races over the giant underwater stones.

I edged along close to the bank, the water almost to my chest. The current's strength pressed me, trying to upend me and sweep me along. I cast a pair of wet flies out and the river gripped them as they sank.

I was edging upstream as I fished, my leg muscles uncomfortable, my booted feet feeling for purchase and position on the microbe-slimy bottom rocks, the dropoff into twelve-foot-deep current inches from my toes.

I didn't like the stretch. I was afraid of it, not just of the danger but of its silence and the unhealthy brown-gray of the current and the way the big rocks loomed like inarticulate beings of ill will under the smooth, racing surface.

I know. Nature is not malevolent. Rocks do not wait. The current does not want to pull a leg then all of you under. The current does not want anything. But that doesn't mean you don't feel it wanting. That doesn't mean you don't feel the rocks waiting. And fish aren't the only things that live in streams. When I was a boy, wading an underwater ledge with three trout on a stringer hanging from my waist, suddenly the current was writhing S-curves by my legs and the stream eel was hitting, biting, tearing at the fish hanging from my stringer. I lost my rod. I was up on the bank gasping, crying, before I even knew what had happened. An eel is an eel, not a malevolent serpent.

A stream eel is no more malevolent than a butterfly. But what you feel is real too.

I was afraid of that stretch so I tried to tell myself there could be no fish in it, but deep, where a cocoon of still water surrounds the base of each boulder, the sides of the underwater rocks are aswarm with crawling aquatic insects and there are fish. It was impossible to punch a cast down to the bottom from where I had no choice but to stand. It was impossible. I didn't like it. I was afraid of it. So, stubbornly, I resolved not to leave this water until I had fished it as thoroughly as I could.

I cast my weighted wet flies in a mortar-shell arc, trying to stab them down through the envelope of fast water into the slow, fecund bottom-currents, but I couldn't tell if I was getting down where I wanted to be or not.

I worked my way up to the head of the run. I tried some downstream throws, long ones, got stuck on a rock, had to break my leader and flies off and lose them to the river. I stood in the fast, brown current rebuilding my leader and attaching a new set of wets. I would not move on until I had given it every chance. On the very next cast a trout slammed one of my flies and I felt the surprising heaviness of the fish's pull in the swift flow. Soon it came up without resisting and, on its side, allowed itself to be dragged over the water to my net, its shining body slapping the current as I cranked it to me.

Then it was evening and I sat sipping a soda under the huge ceiling beams of the main sitting room.

Hunter came over, a bourbon in his hand. He stood over me, his eyes like icy fires. The slabs of muscle that were his forearms, hanging from the short sleeves of his natty shirt, did not fit my image of him as Aristocrat, nor did the rugged hands,

which were rock-steady calm, one holding his glass, the other
hanging at his side. He was showered and shaven and glowing, a
tuft of pink-spotted tissue sticking to his neck where his razor
had nicked him.

He stood there grinning at me as if to say *I am going to sit
down and talk to you and you are going to be charmed.* His eyes
were filled with a scheming, mischievous light. But for the Club
the closest I ever would've gotten to Hunter Sterling King
would've been a TV screen, yet here he was grinning down at
me—I make it sound like it lasted five minutes but it wasn't two
seconds. I wish I could describe the power of the man, the
animal warmth, the talent of command. You couldn't deny
him. To say you perhaps should not have asked him to sit
misses the point. You didn't invite him, he came at you. He
came at you like a train.

He could seem to like you. His smile, when he was winning
you with it, and the piercing eyes, burning with interest, were
irresistible. He sat down and leaning forward as if I were the
most important soul on Earth started questioning me. He
wanted to know what the City Editor of a smalltown news-
paper does. What's the workflow, the pressure to slant stories,
where do you find your best writers . . . I answered his questions and he nodded, nearly biting his lip in his anxiousness to
understand. His eyes, clear as the waters of a Caribbean cove,
were raptly attentive. He was with me unswervingly, stopping
the conversation to clarify a particular point if he wasn't sure
he'd understood, referring back to a point I'd made earlier if it
seemed to tie in, nodding avidly when a detail made sense—
Marian joined us and sat listening. I was tremendously flattered. He wanted my ideas on how the whole system might be
improved. He asked what I'd do if given a free hand. I do have

ideas—I expressed them—I was excited—I'd not talked to anyone, not even Marian, who sympathized the way Hunter King
did just then.

Catching sight of someone he wanted to tell something he
gestured the person over. I sat there holding all the intelligent,
inspired things I wanted to say in while Hunter and the club
member finished their heads-together exchange. He turned
back to me. I was talking again. He was nodding as he listened,
but not as before. He had gotten the information he wanted.
He had his snapshot now. He nodded but he wasn't really
listening. He sat blank-eyed, slack-jawed. He'd formed his picture—it was over. He spoke in an absent, distracted voice of a
certain national columnist, of a mistake she'd once made. He
stared into his glass. It was empty. He had to call Washington.
He was on his feet. He excused himself and disappeared leaving
me feeling as if my pocket had just been thoroughly, charm-
ingly, picked.

At the communal phone in the entry hall, oblivious to who
might be listening, heedless of how he might look, he sat
hunched over the phone hissing into it. Flinging an arm back
and tilting the old wicker chair back against the stairway wall
he would flutter a hand in the air as if physically to route the
conversation away from a point he didn't want made, his eyes
expanding as he listened, then narrowing to snake-slits under
the rococo brows. He prodded and interrogated, cajoled and
flattered, queried, backed off, advanced. I think he just wanted
Washington to know he was there. He just wanted them to
hear his voice. I think it was less what he was saying than that
his presence be ever there, persistent, familiar, expected and
thus somehow necessary. It was a difficult time for him. The
pendulum was swinging against him. The Treasury Secretary

had the President's ear. Fending off a series of challenges to his authority now occupied more of Hunter's time than did the actual discharging of his duties.

He was losing Molly too, though I didn't know this then.

A cousin of hers was moving his family to Anchorage and they were trying to get her to come along. She was thinking about going.

He didn't want her to.

I didn't know any of this then. Looking back I have to admire his will, his energy, whatever it was that drove him to swim forward without complaint into the roil of his troubles.

That Saturday he had climbed to the rock-walled pool and he went up again Sunday, sometimes fishing for it and sometimes just watching the water, sitting on a rock, smoking cigarettes again now after not having touched one since the Army. His tired eyes hallucinated the myriad spots crowding the broad back like sunspots, hundreds and hundreds of dark blotches pressed together on the endless, shining back, each spot with a bright halo around it and the unblinking, cold eye and how it had hung in the water, the waves it had made lapping at its flanks with no more effect than harbor waves breaking against the sides of an anchored carrier.

Sunday when he had to leave without having seen it he was disappointed. He vowed to come up and cast a fly over it one more time before the year was out. And he did. He made it back up that October. I happened to be up myself that autumn weekend—the season was nearly over now and the Club unusually quiet. There weren't a dozen of us in the place.

It was after dinner and I sat dozing over the spy mystery I'd brought along when there he was, looking down at me with a tight-lipped smile.

He asked the angler's immemorial question.

I said yes, I'd had luck, and mentioned a trout-total not more than four in excess of the number I'd actually caught.

I asked him his own question.

He blew out a sigh.

"Not bad," he said. "Not good, not bad. Caught a few."

He sat down, swirled the ice in his glass, and touching the rim to his lips sipped the old man's gratifying, appreciated measure of bourbon.

He was weary. The big face was wan beneath his sportsman's tan, the skin below the eyes grayish and loose.

Standing his glass on the arm of his chair he watched the fire.

"It must be a grind," I ventured.

"It's a test," he said to the fire.

He lifted his bourbon, looked at it, swirled it, stared at it, as if to drink—lowered it, thoughtfully, to the chair arm.

"Did Congress," I ventured, "do pretty much what you wanted?"

In response he gathered himself and with pursed lips shook his head no. His voice came darkly venomous now, low and breathless and tense with righteous fury as he glared at the fire and catechized me:

"Do you know what they did?"

"No sir."

"Do you know what they had the gall—" he was agitated and you could see him struggling to hold his anger in as he sat glowering at the flames "—the *presumption* to do?"

I said nervously that I did not.

He was obviously very angry, the thunderheads scudding low over his brow and his face a dark, unhealthy red, the power in him coiled.

He sat forward, the air bulging outward around him.

"They got us to pretend to be for a bill," he said, "we didn't want. They told us it didn't have a snowball's chance in hell so we could safely come out for it and get credit for the position. Then they passed the goddamn thing!"

I looked at him. The arctic eyes were twinkling. He began to laugh and I joined him, laughing with relief, laughing more than I wanted to be, swept up, carried along yet again. It's hard to explain. I was laughing less at his story than with relief at the discovery that he hadn't been angry. They were like mild black-mail, his power and charm . . .

He gave a derisive snort and stopped laughing, shaking his head and taking a slug of his drink and grinning without mirth at the fire.

The flames rolled up around the big logs as, startlingly, the blaze settled, a shower of sparks scurrying up the flue.

We sat there.

He took a pack of cigarettes out and lit one, with slitted eyes vacuuming in a lungful, exhaled with a hack and looked at it, grimaced, threw it in the fire with an underarm peg.

We sat there by the fire under the century-old beams as his father and grandfather had sat there before us. On the walls hung the proud antlered heads and fish of the past, and there were photos on the walls, angling and gunning poses struck—behind cracked glass—by club members now as dead as the deer and trout they'd briefly survived.

He belongs there, under the huge old beams by the green-gold stream where his ancestors rested from their crimes. He could have been a gentleman-businessman, a gentleman-sports-man, but some twist in the spiral staircase of his genes would not leave him alone.

Sometimes, thinking of Hunter King, I can scarcely recall

what he looked like. It's a trick of the brain's compartments. Then suddenly it's as if he were standing before me, the ruddy, hard face, the woodsman's shoulders and chest, the monumental gravity-center of his presence, up against which and back from which my attempts to get to know him break and ebb without effect . . .

"I promised myself these two days," he sighed to no one in particular, "come hell or high water and by God here I am."

He looked around gratefully at the walls of trophies and framed old photos. He looked up at the wonderful beams of the ceiling. All this was reassuring to him, I think, in a way someone like me can't understand.

We talked about fishing, water we'd known, techniques we'd tried—we talked about gear, how in the next century there will be a single, seamless line from backing to tippet. We derided such advances, knowing we wouldn't live to profit from them, as missing the point of fishing, and, philosophizing, agreed that the primary purpose of fishing is to get outdoors.

"Yes," he sighed. "It's a beautiful sport isn't it?"

"Yes," I said.

And I sighed myself, thinking of streams.

"Just getting outdoors," I found myself saying. "Getting out on all that beautiful water. Even if I don't catch a single fish I'm still satisfied."

The enormity of the lie sobered us both. He stared into the fire. I stared into the fire. We sat there like awed boys waiting for God's hand to strike us. We stared at the coals under the grate: a red-glowing, pulsing landscape of embers. But nothing happened. God does not trouble Himself to strike down individuals. He created a whole random, wonder-filled universe to take care of that on a regular basis.

"My daughter," he said, "wants to go to Alaska."

He sat forward. Scowled.

"She and her cousin and his family," he grimaced. "They're talking about going up next August. He has a crack at some job. Nothing I couldn't get for him here."

Petulantly he blushed. Shook his head.

"I don't want her to go."

Baby rage—insolence of the brat—possessed him. He flushed mightily, as if he would hold his breath 'til he got his way. Then he sat back. You could see him controlling it, clamping it off, handling himself. The muscles of his face relaxed from weariness. His eyes went slack and he was just a tired, discouraged old man.

With a smoke-signal-puff the fire went low. My eyelids were heavy. A couple of members were playing cards over at the far end of the room. That was all. The building was quiet, the cold night still. The fire was going out—it would be up to us to make sure the screen was back in place before we went up. On tables and the arms of chairs stood ashtrays, half-finished drinks, riffled-through magazines, half-full coffee cups.

Fishing season was over. The place would be virtually empty now until deer season. I yawned. Smoke hung under the vast ceiling. The card players had finished and were walking around turning off lamps. They waved, mumbling goodnight, and left us to what was left of our fire. The rest of the room was washed silver now by the moonbeams streaming down through the big windows and French doors. The moonlight lit the long, empty room with a ghostly brightness, a cold and hoary stillness that fell strangely upon the deserted chairs and sofas and on the great antlered heads on the walls. Suddenly the room was of a size I couldn't determine. It seemed a different room, something from another time. I was sleepy, I know, I was imagining things, but the feeling gripped me all the same. It was as if I had journeyed by mistake to this ancient, unknown hall of deer heads and ghastly light. And it seemed, as I watched, that a procession would come in. Some nameless, soulless train was going to enter, a ragtag and endlessly old, noble company of hoarbearded wizards, stately stags, cherubs, skill-faced warriors, white-haired virgins, a fat boy carrying a plate . . . it was an illusion. I'd imagined it. The room was a room. I was who I am. Hunter stirred and straightening himself leaned forward, a hand grasping either chair arm.

I got out of my chair. One of us said something about putting the fire-screen back. One of us did it. I was enormously tired. We climbed the creaking staircase in that ringing, otherworldly light.

And that was the last I saw of him until spring.

I read about him in the newsmagazines over the winter. I would stare in fascination at the photos of him in a business suit and tie whom I saw, in the flesh, only in that tattered hat or one of the plaid shirts he sported when he would lower himself, after the day's fishing rigors, into one of the sitting room's threadbare chairs.

He was a battler.

I know he worked terrifically hard. I don't think his failures were ever for lack of trying. He strove in some ugly arenas, places where they trick and cuff you, and he was down more than once but his head always came bobbing up bravely like an infant's. Innocence could always flow back into the blue of those astonishing eyes. He could refresh himself, shake his woes off and forget, whatever the defeat, whatever the cruelty he had committed. I think you need that ability to survive in the world he knew. I don't know that world. The picture I'm giving you is incomplete. I know next to nothing of his life in that white city. I have no idea what he had to go through to achieve what he did. I don't even know what he achieved. Back when I thought this would be a full-fledged study of him I talked to some people, and one individual credited Hunter King with the last stretch of genuine Mideast peace. Another said he'd never had an original thought in his life and got as far as he did only through pure grit. A third said he couldn't be comfortable unless he had several false promises out at any given moment and at least some of his staff working—to his knowledge only— at cross purposes to each other.

A fourth person told me no one would ever know the number of times Hunter King had given of himself and of his wealth in complete anonymity to bolster worthy organizations and launch—and rescue—the careers of men and women who couldn't possibly have been of use to him.

I don't know. I'm not qualified to judge.

My own work advanced when I was made Managing Editor of our little daily, and Sean fought his way through kindergarten.

It was a harsh winter—record-low stretches, blizzard after blizzard. Marian and I worked hard, enjoying it for the most part, but it gets hectic sometimes with the boys. I took care of them for a week when she had to be in Chicago and by the end of that seven days my eyes were glazed I can tell you.

One howling, sub-zero evening I got my tackle out and took inventory, categorizing and ordering my flies by pattern and size, tidying the pockets of my vest, cleaning and oiling and rewinding my reels. I tried to show things—explaining them— to Sean but he showed no interest. He preferred television, torturing the cat, anything to the complexity of equipment I thought he should find so fascinating. It snowed. It sleeted. It rained ice. Cars shimmied down the streets near-missing each other between the walls of snow the plows had built and the wind shrieked down the streets and whined and buzzed in our old windows' weather stripping and I passed my cold to Marian who passed it to Sean who passed it to Richard. There was nothing to do but sneeze and bundle up and drive in to work in the freezing darkness while you waited, patiently, for that moment when, as if weightless, it blows down out of the perfumy air to perch on your hand's skin, its tiny body and tiny outsized head palest yellow, upswept wings, jauntily erect above the thorax, filled with light, membraneous, net-veined and translucent like flakings of finest confectionery.

Holding her on your palm you look at her, the thread-thin, champagne-pale legs—twice-jointed—working ineffectually and the tubular abdomen curling up, and up, like the tail of a groggy scorpion as she tries to lay her eggs.

When you lift your eyes to the warm evening the air is everywhere filled with her sisters fluttering, twittering, spiralling against the sky, and there's a splash, then another, then splashes everywhere.

Your hands are so unsteady from joy and your heart is pumping so hard with anticipation that assembling your rod and threading it with line and getting a fly tied on happens too infuriatingly slowly, like dream slow-motion.

I love to fish. I wouldn't change the life I have with Marian and the boys for anything but the one thing I do miss from my going-in-circles bachelorhood is the fishing—I fished three times as much then as I do now. I'm lucky to have had the opportunity. I'll never have that freedom again (I wouldn't want it), but at least I'm fortunate enough once to have had it. I can remember the times. I can see the settings. I can hear the sounds and feel the textures, the weather changes. I find my memories neither dim with the passing of the years nor lose their power to comfort. No matter how often I take them out, turning them in the light, to look at them, their power does not diminish.

When I was in school I could never understand what people like Wordsworth and Hemingway meant about memory being able to sustain you.

But that was when I was young.

five

At dusk in the Arkansas Ozarks I have watched the White River, that runs from Bull Shoals south past Little Rock practically to the Mississippi, rise with a swiftness you can imagine, as you stare at the swirling waters, is Nature knowing about us and not liking what She knows, not wanting us here on Her planet.

In the sweet windless evening I stood at the currents' edge looking at my feet as the river's lappings, glinting with the light from our campfire, drew near my toes. You could watch, so quickly was the water coming up, the river's rim creep, pebble by pebble, toward your toes.

I'd gone down with friends and we'd rented a flatboat. That was the summer after college, the only one of those you get. Now at day's end miles upstream at the dam they were releasing water and I watched the river's quivery edge nearing my toes as the water rose and in the shadows you could hear the sucking, splashing current that had been so placid that afternoon when stepping out of the boat with the sun on your back you had waded about in sneakers in the bright sunshine flipping your pattern anywhere and landing ten-inchers under the furnace sun.

In the coming on of night the flow speeds to a rush the dangerous suck and gargle of which you can hear, though you can't see it, from shore. The transformed river is carrying along debris, branches, even big logs. One does not take a boat out. When peals of nervous laughter glide by in the twilight you stand at the water's edge cupping your hands around your shouts: "Hello! Are you all right? Hello!" But whatever boat it is—was—is swept downstream out of earshot in seconds and there is nothing, when you think about it, you could have done.

I stripped naked. Bracing myself, testing each move before making it, I worked my way out into the shuddering current and got my bare body wedged in among some rocks.

Closing my eyes I let go, relaxing every muscle. The current trembled against my nakedness like a thousand kneading fingers massaging me, with relentless power reducing my baby-helpless, rock-wedged body to laughter.

In the morning out on that same water, pokey-slow now in the dawn still, primal cliffs slide by as we float. Virgin stands of forest flow by. The strange, utter silence of the wilderness. Hogs slide by where there are farms, waddling out along the gravel bars to grunt, snuffle and root . . .

Near Phoenix, against the pellucid, aquamarine bottom of the hole I'd spent an hour looking into on Oak Creek, either bank plunging to cup the water like a pair of great votive hands, the trout lay quiescent. They lay inert, hanging still, each with its shadow motionless beneath it, so that there was nothing to do but to be still, like them, and stare at them.

Peaks of rock thousands of feet high are reflected in the blue-gray Wyoming lakes. Big ones, subs, cruise about where the mountain streams tumble out into the wide water flats, and in the lightning-quick rock-cluttered little creeks the quick little ones are so fast in their takes you need to strike before you feel the hit, strike the instant you see the flash.

All along the stately limestone runs of southern Pennsylvania they stand on their heads nosing the lush green underwater vegetation for bugs.

Their tails, in rows, stick out of the current comically.

Wading the dangerous Madison with the orange-pink sun staring across the Montana sky at the phosphoreal moon you hold your fly up to the last of the light supplicatingly, trying yet again to get tiny strand to go through tiny eye.

The times you have had are clear. They are in you. They don't solve problems and ought not to be dwelt upon but they're there, always, to steady you, to give you your bearings back when you've lost them, to give you a sense of the world as a place capable of peace.

In Connecticut when we were living there the Shepaug, the Hollenbeck, Glen Run, the Farmington. Those bright-washed mornings just before late-April daylight savings used to come in, when the sun would glow up out of the hills at five. That stretch along the Farmington above the old forge, that tremendous, forest-mirroring lake of a pool above the ruins of the old dam and furnace tower, where in the deserted quiet of sunrise a beaver is paddling, its wake spreading behind it as it swims, matter-of-factly, out of the sunshine into the shadows of the forest guarding the far shore.

When the White Drake hatch is on in the Connecticut Berkshires to be out on Waitelotte Pond in a canoe is like tearing the top off a box of chocolates and forgetting your diet. They're everywhere, slapping the water near and far in the warm mists 'til you get giddy, drifting to and fro in your canoe and hauling them out as fast as you can put them back.

As a worm the White Drake wriggles to the surface to writhe, painfully from the looks of it, free of its skin. Out across the water thousands of pairs of chalk-white wings are struggling torturously, half-trapped half-free. That's when the fish like to take them, big rainbows surging up. You plop a White Wulff down and the hit comes in seconds. The mists are thickening in the darkening air. There's a coolness suddenly— it's night, but you aren't thinking about that. You said you would be home by nine but it isn't going to happen.

Those that survive, wrenching free of their wormskin to hop a few times on the water and fly in stuttery spirals up into the dim, are taken by the birds. The birds explode from the trees to—in mid-flight—swallow the erratically fluttering insects in a gulp.

After an afternoon of complete frustration on Rabbit Creek in the Great Smokies you hurl your line too far on purpose, messily, straight up the miniature stream's center. You make the cast uphill, visibly so, the water stepping away from you up the mountainside pool by pool like a terraced stairway going away through the forest.

You make the senseless cast out of boredom and anger way upstream into a corner of a pool just below a little chute of a falls, and you think the weight you feel must be your bellying line, but it isn't—even at seventy feet the locus of resistance can be felt as not static. Barely legal, hooked on the afternoon's last annoyed, sloppy cast, your diminutive trophy is to be waded up to, creeled, and carried back to camp for showing off—sheepishly—to her whom you'd planned to impress with a stringer of mighty ones.

It looked pathetically small at the center of the pan.

She was appreciative though, and the taste was wonderful.

That evening we made love on the blanket I'd brought from the tent to spread beside the fire, and she was saying, turning her face from me: "Please, please do that, oh please do that," as in our friendship and lust under the trees' shadows we called Sean out of the stars.

six

Fishing didn't interest Sean but I wanted him to learn. He was only six and had plenty of time but I was anxious to see him start. I wanted to see him catch his first trout. I wanted him to know the pleasure of stalking them and being frustrated. I wanted him to know how mistaken and fine—and like each other—life and fly fishing can be.

So I took him down to Old Man Buchanan's ponds, where we stock big rainbows, and because I wanted him to be interested I paid him no attention.

He wandered off, looking out from under the visor of his too-big Phils hat.

Dazzlingly the spiderwebs hanging in the soaked grasses caught the morning light. The sun was warming and rising through the rain-streaked woods and here in the glade where

Elkins Buchanan's four ponds lay in a row, linked by a succession of spillways, the air was moist-fresh and new. I filled my lungs, felt the air's cool on my face, with my eyes enjoyed the fine hurt of the brilliant before-breakfast sunlight and with my heart revelled at being miles from any office.

It had been a swamp, impassable and mosquito-breeding until Buchanan had remade it. Plotting each stage from excavation through grading and sluice-construction to planting he had personally overseen the project from beginning to end.

Into ponds One and Two he had ordered boulders to be lowered.

They stood about twenty feet out, half-submerged, slate-gray presences.

To attract insects he oversaw the planting of shrubs and bushes and for attractiveness scattered a handful of Norway maples, their leaves pastel green now—soon to go to summer's verdance—and in October a flaming, dramatic scarlet against the blue.

Beyond ponds Three and Four in the meadow's western corner where the evening shadows always pool first in summer, a willow, mournful and majestic, bends her many lovely necks low.

I feel good down there. The place comforts me. It was a swamp when he started, and now it's tidy and quite beautiful. The big rocks stand in the water because Elkins Buchanan caused them to stand in the water. There are four ponds and not five or three because Elkins Buchanan said four. The trees are maples and a willow because he decreed it.

Kneeling in the sweet grasses I dug in the loam and they wriggled as they recoiled from the light.

Sean was trying to climb across one of the sluices. His

Phillies hat is too big for him and he wears it constantly, the visor down practically over his eyes shadowing his face and requiring him, when he wants to see something, to lift his chin. He loves to fight. He once said of his best friend, Pete, "Pete's my best friend but I don't understand why he doesn't like to fight more." When he fights his hat falls off and lies there. Afterward he picks it up and puts it back on. He sleeps in it and his mother and I allow him to forbid us to wash it.

I caught one, its slime-moist coils trying to wind around my fingers, and carrying it to the water's edge threw it in.

I watched it sink until fast as light a fish hit it.

I went back, at no point looking at Sean, and got another. He was watching now. He was interested. I could feel his eyes on me, following me as I carried the worm back to the water. As it sank two fish swirled. I sensed him standing behind me but did not say anything or turn to look.

I went back to my digging place and got a memorable ugly one and carried it back to the water and tossed it in. We watched it sink, squirming, slowly, as it turned, curvingly, over itself and around itself as it descended into the microbe-green still.

The trout was a streak of yellow. It hit the writhing meat and with a tail-flash was gone. I said nothing. Sean stood staring out from under his oversized visor at the water. I went back and got more, yanking their accordion-contracting shapes from the darkness. I got a handful and hurrying back threw them all in.

The water was a cauldron of obsessed trout flashing up and swimming through each other to snap their jaws shut—some of them in their excitement on worms not even there. Surfaceward they flashed diving the instant their jaws smacked shut, big ones and little ones nearly running into others flying up as they all swerved and dived.

The water was peaceful again now and while I did not look at him I could feel his presence beside me and sense his curiosity as he watched the inscrutable green. I said nothing. I turned and walked a little way off, surreptitiously turning to peek.

He was standing at the water's edge looking down at where they had been, his child's thighs, above the soiled puddles of his socks, muscular and defined.

Marian had brought Richard down. She stood him in the warming grasses and he worked on his walking, considering, swaying, and when the window of coordination occurred taking quick steps like one of those toy people with moving legs that totter down an inclined plane. His chubby legs disobeyed him and he sat, surprised. Lowering his head he pushed to his feet, swayed, grinning crookedly, and blurted the four-letter word he'd heard me shout a few days previously upon hammering my thumb instead of the nail-head I was aiming for. The first time he'd come out with it Marian and I had fairly pounced. Asking him where he'd heard that and admonishing him never *ever* to say such a word we were only teaching him, we realized too late, the mysterious syllable's power.

She scooped him up and threw him against the sky and caught him and we walked back up through the cool of the woods to the clubhouse.

I did terribly that morning, missing several good fish in the first hour. Soon my frustration at wading, tinkering with flies, trudging the bank, casting, unhooking my fly from myself, was so fierce, so complete, that I began to move in a vagueness, casting without authority, scanning the water without hope,

hurrying when caution was called for and lingering over situa-
tions I knew I should abandon, listlessly presenting my fly to
the same dead stretches again and again . . .

Lunch back at the Club with Marian was a quick hello-
goodbye. I was irritated, with not a trout to my credit. I was
desperate to get back out on the water. I was the fly angler at
his worst: preoccupied, compulsive. I pecked her turned-away
cheek as Richard quietly said "Fuck" to himself over her shoulder and she tried, with a hand, to get Sean's shirttail in.

Then I was back out in it, the water's differing speeds and
the way the light varied dizzying me as I stood waist-deep in the
flow, garlanded with equipment, plying my line. The pool I was
fishing was sheltered by a coppice of laurel. Reflected off the
water the sunshine played against the bushes' deep-shiny leaves:
a changing tunefulness of lights. A fish lived here, but when he
drifted up he saw something he didn't like. In a smooth move
he angled back down, out of sight.

I changed flies and caught him. It must have been the
change of flies. Do you think so?

Fly anglers believe trout can distinguish a size-twenty fly
from a size-eighteen in the identical pattern. They believe trout
can tell natural peacock quill from peacock quill dyed red, can
perceive the difference between a pair of wings angled at ten
o'clock and wings standing at the vertical. If I switch flies and
take a fish where previously I have had no success I take it for
granted the change caused the hit. The waiting fish saw something marginally different and struck.

Indeed trout can probably discern a thirty-degree variance
in wing angle or a sixteenth-of-an-inch difference in a fly's body
length. But what then of the hook? Naked curve-and-barb
shaped unlike anything in the stream and accounting for a full

third of your fly's overall area, the hook doesn't get much attention from the fly scientists—but if trout can see color gradations and distinguish minor differences in size and texture then surely the hook, protruding dark, unnaturally shaped and obvious into the water below your floating fly's silhouette, must make a terrific difference.

What if the hit is conditional less upon your fly's size or shape than upon whether or not, as your pattern passes over the waiting trout, some trick of light, angle, or both happens to render the sore-thumb hook momentarily invisible?

What then of all our intense design-debates?

Maybe the fish saw my hook the first time. Maybe some trick of light, the second time, rendered the hook invisible. Maybe the fish saw the hook and struck anyway, irrationally, just as we anglers are driven to debate irrelevant minutiae. Maybe just as the fly tyer ignores the effect the hook surely must have so the fish, just as irrationally, ignores the hook.

Wiping my brow I waded into darkness. The branches of the pines closed over me. They lay everywhere in the shadows, their rises soft. I went to a light tippet and staying low, hiding behind bushes, took and released three, the soporific droning of the insects and the motions of the current and the slight breeze moving through the trees filling my mind as if forest, sky, and stream were in my mind as well as outside it.

It was late. I was tired. I stood in a reedy puddle at the edge of the last, dark pool of the day. Sunbeams penetrated the black water a little way, stirring like rustling quivers of arrows of light, but the rest was darkness. Gathering in line I walked my pattern a short distance over whatever unimaginable bottom.

I looked at the gray rocks while I waited. Lime-green mosses lived on them. At the water's edge grew clumps of Indian fig, their pale-yellow, fragilely offered blossoms delicate-looking atop their stout, prickly stems.

I gathered in a portion more of line, my fingers working like the arthritic digits of a miser. I waited. Nothing happened. Slowly, evenly, I crimped more inches of line into my fingers. My eyes widened. With a savage flash I struck, my rod whipping back beside my shoulder and my line pointing down— taut—into the blackness. I started to muscle the fish up and it was in instant revolt, exploding the gloom, breaking the shadows into spectacular bright showers of spray, whacking its tail against the water, diving deep, swimming back and forth tugging my line back and forth through the water, breaching again, shaking its head mightily and finning the water into more silvery upshowerings. At last, bested—revived and released, it swam tiredly down out of sight.

I reeled in and put childish things away and turned back through the late-afternoon light walking the forest trail around under my booted feet like a treadmill, inattentive to my surroundings, ready for a shower.

I was weary, climbing the porch steps. I'd worked hard. I lost my balance like Richard when he walks, almost fell then had my foot on the next step. I was going up when the door burst wide. A club member I hardly knew rushed at me.

"Did you hear?"

I was tortured with fear—Marian and the boys!

He stared at me, the shock still fresh on his face.

"He's out!" he practically shouted.

"Who's out? What do you mean?"

"Hunter King! It's all over the news! He's quit!"

seven

He'd been canned. A series of encroachments on his authority—meetings held without him, statements made without his
being consulted—had driven him to a session with the President. Earnestly, his hands trying to shape, in the Oval Office
sunlight, each point as he strove to make it, he outlined what
would have to change for him to stay. The response was no eye
contact and a blur of half-sentences to the effect that it was
unfortunate, but if he felt it was time for him to go, then
perhaps it was.

The Treasury Secretary had wanted him out—he was out.

He came up with Molly. We greeted him with a certain
hesitation. He looked tired, the eyes tired, the light in them
wary and low, defeat trying to multiply in him like a virus. The
semicircle of white hair around the base of the big head was

longer than I'd ever seen it, thick and wisping as it curled down the back of his sun-roughened neck. He flashed us his usual smile. But when he turned away you could see it in the eyes—a tiredness and the least, mad glint of disbelief.

Molly stayed by his side like a mysterious nurse.

I couldn't stop looking at her. I managed to avoid staring but I was powerless not to steal glance after glance. Her cool, wistful grace—a navy sweater draped from the aristocratically correct shoulders—mesmerized me. I took look after look. If her father moved off from the group and she turned to be with him I would find an excuse to move to where I could see her. I would decide I wanted coffee I didn't want, just to be able to make a pass by her. I can see her, the strange, thin lips, the perfectly careless way her sweater hung from her shoulders, the gold-gray, untame hair—she never experimented with different hairstyles. I'm sure it never occurred to Molly King to take five dresses from the closet and try each twice or to sit before the mirror, head turned, to experiment with earrings or fluffing her hair one way and not liking it impatiently to swat it different.

The four of us played cards after dinner, Hunter's dismissal like a fifth, foreign presence at the table. As I lay down each card I was trying not to appear to be looking at her.

The muscled chest lifted and subsided under the pink and green of his shirt. His hand held his cards fanned out. Only the big chest moved, the faintest whistle audible when a breath escaped his nostrils. In the ashtray beside him the butts of three cigarettes lay in a smoking wash of ash . . . he didn't seem to want another. He sat there, breathing.

"Dad?"

"Hm?"

"It's your play."

"Yes," he said. "Let's see here."

He made a decision and played a card. Molly nibbled at a fingernail. To see her biting her nail—teeth bared—unnerved me. She bit, not daintily, at her nail as she regarded her cards. She shut her hand, fanning it open again and going back to worrying at the nail. I was staring at her. I was irrational. Marian's leg touched mine under the table. It stayed there.

At the next table a young investment banker, his slicked-back hair suave in the lamplight, was locked in a cigar-billowing battle of stud poker with some compatriots. There were the grumbles and good-natured growls of men playing cards.

Molly couldn't decide what card to play. The gray eyes considered. She took her time—always that aloofness . . . if you didn't know her you might have thought it was uncertainty. To see the long fingers dancing over her cards you might have thought she was indecisive. But I don't think that's what it was. I don't think it was indecisiveness. I think it was her iron insistence, given the world as it is instead of some way we might like it, on not letting life teach her any lessons she didn't want to learn.

Eternally the trophy trout of yesteryear swirled and dove about the high walls. Antlers high, nostrils alert, the prize deer of another era stared at the challenge of some unchanging horizon. Big night moths came thudding at the screens.

The banker flipped his cards.

"They bear no relation to each other," he growled. "Take it."

He pushed his chair back and winked—it was fast—at Molly who'd been looking at him.

She blushed quickly lowering her eyes.

It was demure and not particularly flustered, with downcast lashes.

Hunter saw it. I saw him see it. His eyes gulped. It's the only way I can describe it. He looked like a forsaken little boy. He stared at her, needing her, gazing pathetically at his daughter.

She took the trick. The rest were ours. We said goodnight. In the front hall Hunter loomed at Marian taking her hand and kissing her cheek with profound ceremony. He turned to me and taking my hand and gripping my wrist, his face close, started to talk.

He made a speech, putting his face into mine to say how glad he was, how much our friendship, the evening, meant to him. He couldn't think of anyone he'd rather have been with. He said he looked forward to many such evenings. He looked forward to fishing together, to being with us, to working together to build our club into something truly extraordinary— his eyes were moist—his grip did not slacken as he thanked me, grasping my wrist. He wanted to know if we ever got down to Washington. If we ever did we should be sure and drop in on him. He was going to keep an office there. I must look him up. He could show me around.

Then wearily he was ascending the creaky stair with his daughter, going up behind, flashing us a shrug of a smile.

"It must be hard on him," I said hopping on a foot.

Marian turned the covers down and climbed in. She lay back against her pillow as I got my trousers off and hung them up and got my pajamas on and climbed in.

Pulling the lamp-chain I put us in darkness.

The stream was too far away to hear over on this side of the sprawling old building, and outside our window the summer night was quiet. No cricket sang. The darkness was perfectly still. Yet the night felt alive with the presence of the forest and all the creatures breathing and stirring in the mountainside wilderness.

Rolling against me she slipped an arm under mine. She has always had a ravenous metabolism and is warm, always burning off energy, even in repose. Her voice and breath were startling so near my ear:

"Is she as attractive to you as I am?"

I froze, pointedly in my guilt, and sighed.

"You're talking about Molly King."

"That's right."

"There's nothing," I mumbled.

I wanted to sound sleepy.

I felt her go alert.

"Joe what are you saying?"

"I'm saying," I said, putting as much weariness into my voice as I could, "what I mean. I'm not even sure I know what you're talking about."

I burrowed my cheek in the pillow.

"I'm talking about the fact that she fascinates you. You're obviously attracted to her. I'm just curious."

A wash of pale moonlight spilled across the wall.

"She doesn't fascinate me."

I could feel her thinking in the warm June blackness.

"Joe?"

"Hm?"

"Are you telling me the truth?"

Her goodness was intolerable. Of course I wasn't telling her the truth. How could she expect someone who wasn't telling her the truth to tell her the truth? I didn't want to think. I didn't know myself. I wanted to be asleep.

"It's nothing," I said.

"Do you think she's beautiful?"

"She's attractive," I said. "I think she's attractive. That's all."

"But do you think she's beautiful?"

I made my voice groggy.

"No."

"But you do find her attractive."

Her arm was like a perfumed toll bar lying across me. Feigning a sleepy toss I extricated myself. She rolled on her side away from me and we lay in silence, not touching, the darkness tense—taut—with the conversation we weren't having.

eight

The chauffeur, a large person, whose mashed nose reminded me of my favorite TV villain, helped his master unfold from the long car and into the steaming daylight where, blinking, Elkins Buchanan leaned on his cane and with a steady quiver shook hands with us as we filed across the parking area to pay our respects.

He hardly ever came up anymore. Our excitement was genuine—he had drawn breath in the same century as Napoleon. He had seen the coming of the automobile, the airplane, the radio. He had founded the Club, bought the land, built the building, drained and tamed the swamp—it was as if God Himself had arrived wearing a tweed jacket and bright yellow bowtie.

Above the mottled forehead, off which the skin was peeling

in shreds like flaking paint, the few remaining strands of his white hair lifted and waved on the day's breezes with the swaying motion of some delicate undersea plant.

His eyes twinkled—red-veined, aware—but the set of the mouth was wrong. The mouth was frozen. The mouth looked dead, as if he were halfway out of this life already, the eyes still here, the mouth already crossed over.

His man picked him up and carried him down the trail to the water. His director's chair was set up and he allowed himself to be lowered into it. He took his rod—offered with a deferential bow—and began to catch fish. The top half of him worked fine. His wrist commanded his rod sharply and his fly floated light as a breeze-wafted mote onto the current's subtleties. When a fish struck the old face did not change. Rod flashed up to set hook and scrawny tweed arm lifted to control shuddering bamboo parabola as the victim splashed and scurried about trying to get safe and then, rolling on its side, was drawn near the rocky bank. The chauffeur, squatting, would net it, free the hook, and according to how he was instructed release it or blackjack it and drop it in the antique wicker creel, shaped like the stern of a galleon, that he wore on his hip.

I stood in the small audience scattered down through the trees. When there was nothing to do the chauffeur stood at semi-attention, his eyes following his master's fly.

I stole closer, down through the trees. I could hear the faint *whish* of the line. With each hit the ancient arm flashed up and struggled, the face showing no change in expression. When his fly had been returned to him, without hesitation he conjured it out to a new location on the turbulent waters. He knew the currents so well he could go right to each place where there was a fish and go there, from his chair, at just the right angle and with just the right float. I stepped a couple of steps nearer down through the trees.

I could hear something. I didn't know what it was . . . I listened. I heard it again—thought it was the stream, water-noise—but it was his voice . . . he was saying something, talking to himself as he fished . . . I stepped forward, cupping my ears. What did God know? He hooked a trout and his arm flew up. His voice was scarcely audible over the noises of the brook.

"Why you little son of a bitch!"

With a whip of the wrist Elkins Buchanan lashed his line out once more.

"The little bastards," he mused.

He touched the currents' hiding places sitting there in his director's chair on that slate-gray slab conjuring his line out before him, behind him, and before him. He was onto another one. Its broad back and dorsal fin showing black-green it barged to the pool's tail. It was going over the rocks—he'd lose it! Standing in the trees we watched. Giving a pull the old man lurched in his chair—suddenly his chair was on two legs instead of four. His man leapt forward—several of us cried out. He was going over! With a trick none of us had seen, a stupendous trick, a trick I wouldn't have thought of in a thousand years, he turned the fish and was safe again in his chair.

"You little *bastard!*" he chortled.

His driver cleaned those they'd kept. Elkins Buchanan allowed himself to be lifted from his chair and carried up through the trees riding noncommittally in his man's arms like a motion-mesmerized infant.

Set down on his feet on the pebbly flat of the parking area he gripped his cane and willfully negotiated the remaining steps to his car.

With a wave to those of us lingering in the hazy sunlight he turned, ducking his head, and crumpled into the back seat.

The door clicked shut. He leaned back, letting his head fall against the rich plush, his face indistinct in the murk of the thick protective glass as he stared out at us.

I think people who fish for trout with flies get strange. My sister-in-law for instance, studying a road map one time, trying to figure how to get from where she was in New Jersey to where she wanted to go in Connecticut, referred annoyedly to the expressways around New York City as "this snarl of back-lashed monofilament."

Elkins Buchanan, fishing from his chair, cackling as he put the hook to each next "little son-of-a-bitch," was loony as a god, and another of our members, Dr. Sierra, who will stand all afternoon in the same spot fishing for a single rising trout, trying every fly he owns, tells me that before he goes onto the stream he never spends less than an hour laying out his equipment and with his wife's help going down the checklist he keeps (like pilot and co-pilot before takeoff) to make sure tweezers and scissors and file and floatant and bug dope and split shot and thermometer and flies and leaders and tippet spools are in proper condition and organized exactly as he wants them.

As you drift into sleep your mind can feel the tight-trembling way your line shuddered when you were fighting that day's big one. I can't remember my Social Security Number but I can tell you the fly I used, can describe to you the precise way the currents flowed, could point out exactly where, on the Oregon stream I won't name, the big steelhead surged up to hook itself when I was out there seventeen summers ago. But fly fishing isn't any stranger than anything else I guess. The changing line of all the casts you've made, the one you're making, and those you've yet to make is no stranger than the unfurling line of all your days and evenings—gentle, lavender-breezy twilights—along the stream.

nine

When Molly King told her father she'd decided to move to Alaska it seemed at first that he would take the news tranquilly. In a calm tone he asked her if she were sure. She said she was sure. He asked her if she had thought it through. She held the telephone away from her ear, slumping like a wrestler stealing a second's rest. Yes she said.

Then, he said, he wished her well.

There was silence between them now on the line.

He said it made sense.

She said she'd thought it through. There was the echoing ringing of the open line between them. He wished her luck. She thanked him. He said he hoped she wouldn't mind a visitor now and then. She said he and her mother should try and get up just as often as they could.

The silence lasted longer this time, as if walls were being pushed back, zooming out away from her in all directions as she sat holding the receiver.

He asked her if she had her ticket. Summer could be a tough time to get a ticket if you waited until the last minute. She said she had her ticket. He said be sure and confirm your reservation.

Between them the open line, enormous, like a vast, darkened cavern, stirred with electronic impulses—fragments of other people's conversations . . .

She asked if he were all right.

He said of course he was. He asked her if she'd like to go fishing again before she left. She closed her eyes, said yes. They agreed on a weekend. They said goodbye. As she hung up she experienced an upwelling of rage that she endured, staring at her hand resting on the telephone, and bore the strain of and threw the strain of forward into her rod as she stood in the river in the late-afternoon light hurling her casts low against the wind to where the soft dimples formed and disappeared on the current flowing past the stony bank, with a ripple and swirl, in the shade of a row of alders. Her arm powered forward and her tight-looped casts rolled out low. It looked like they were taking midges, drifting up not quite to the surface to open their jaws, fan their gills, and finically inhale. The visor of her cap pulled down against the westering sun and her booted legs planted against the river's push she loaded her rod and unsprung it hurtling her line out over the sun-glittery currents into the corridor of shadow where the trees stood.

They had asked me to fish with them and for most of the afternoon the three of us had been fishing separately but now we'd come together and were standing together in the current,

Molly casting to the kiss-rises along the rocky shoreline, Hunter and I watching.

I hadn't planned to be at the Club that weekend. Marian was working on a brief and had announced she would need to work that Saturday and probably most of Sunday so I'd been planning to be home with the boys, but that Friday at dinner she was quiet, her thinking-finger tapping the table by her plate, and when we'd cleared and were in the kitchen rinsing dishes and loading the dishwasher she said why not see if Sean's and Richie's grandparents would take them, then I could go fishing.

I didn't say anything. We were busy with plates and pots and I felt uncomfortable and beside me the red-brown of her hair shone in the fluorescent light as she worked and I knew she'd decided that she wanted whatever was going to happen to happen. I was scared and excited. I said as offhandedly as I could well all right, maybe I will. And the next morning driving out of the city wondering if Molly would be there I felt guilty and angry and excited, and as the roads I was taking narrowed and the forests grew higher crowding in close overhead as my old car slowed and started to strain with the climb into the mountains, guilt fell away like the cities far below and I went on edge. My nerves went on edge like a stalked beast's. People were finishing their coffee and moving around getting ready to go fishing when I arrived and forth through the dining-room doorway Hunter strode rubbing his hands together, his shirtsleeves rolled up above his elbows. Behind him she was looking me in the eye as he let out with a shout of delight to see me and gripped my shoulder and pumped my hand chuckling for God's sake hurry up and get ready we don't have all day. Behind him the dun-gray, secret eyes were looking into mine.

Now morning and afternoon had vanished in a blur of

fishing hours and night—truth-time—would soon be on us. The three of us stood together in the current's eternal pressure as the sun went low in the sky and she was casting into the wind to the difficult rises in the shade of the shoreline trees.

The evening was glass-pure. A sharp, steady breeze blew through the canyon the forest made along the river. The trees' boughs waved, falling and lifting with the moving air as if to some ceaseless, huge-breathing music.

The sun burned low and white-blinding at us.

We couldn't see her fly when it landed. We edged closer to her side, squinting, shading our eyes.

I couldn't see.

I took my sunglasses off. The shadow was less now but the sunlight was blinding. I put them back on. Now the sunlight was better but the shadows were practically impenetrable. Hunter and I stood in the current trying to spot for her. You couldn't see her eyes behind the double-Polaroids she wore against the sun. Being near her gave me a floating, lifting feeling like what the wind was doing to the trees.

The fish were rising to within an inch of the surface to inhale pupal husk, water, and struggling emerger as fastidiously as dowagers sipping tea. As they turned back toward the depths, expelling the air they'd taken in, dainty signature bubbles were left behind on the moving surface.

Her fly flew off the water and came sailing at us as she struck and missed.

"You're too fast with it," he said.

"I can't see my fly."

"When you see the rise, wait. They don't take it in right away. It's a slow inhale. You see the rise and you wait. *Then* you strike."

"How can I wait if I can't see it?"

"Count to three."

She struck. Her line came flying back at us.

"*Damn* it."

"I'm telling you Molly you're too fast."

"Well maybe if you'd leave me *alone!*"

Hunter King folded his arms. He stared down at the water swirling about his boots.

Without lifting his head he lifted his eyes. Under the salt-and-pepper brows the snapper eyes were watching as she fired another low cast into the wind.

"Okay," I saw his silently moving lips say as his eyes followed her fly. "Good. That's good."

She did not strike.

Her fly was in, or near, the jaws of a trout.

She waited.

Hunter bit his lip to keep quiet.

She flicked her rod up, stripping in line, and her rod dipped and there was a heavy, living weight straining against her in the cold-flowing run.

She hauled back pulling the fish away from the bank out into the main current and there was a storm-shower of spray.

"You can talk now," she said without looking at him.

"Don't let it past those rocks."

"I know."

"See what I mean?"

"I *know* Dad."

"It's a good one," he said happily.

It came floating toward us and he was coaching her.

"Easy now. Here it comes. Hang on. That's a beautiful fish Moll. Hang on now. Easy does it."

Carefully netted, silver-lavender, the luminous sleekness of the body elegant in the curve of mucous-glistening back, the fish stared at the bright air with an eye.

He held it up and we admired it, then he let it go and we watched it flash away in the current.

"Bigger ones than that live here," he said holding his rod under his arm as he checked her fly and leader for her. "We'll come up sometime and go night-fishing."

The river's might pressed our boots against our legs, the flow sweeping over the big bottom rocks as the whole enormous, moving volume of water poured against us.

"Molly?"

"Yes?"

He leaned toward her.

"Would you like to? To come up once more before you leave and try some night-fishing?"

She had taken her line back from him and was running her leader through her fingers, looking for flaws.

"I don't think I can," she said.

He was leaning toward her.

"Don't you want to?"

She shook her head no.

He turned and was swinging his shoulders as he splashed away from us.

"Come on boys and girls," he threw over a shoulder as he waded, "time to get back."

Where the bottom shallowed out the current broke apart into many currents meandering and crisscrossing through themselves and he waded about lifting stones from the water and turning them over to show us the pincered, crawly life clinging to the rocks' undersides.

He tied something on and plopping it into the pockets picked up a chubby brook trout. We'd keep it for breakfast, he decided. Along the bank below the parking area he slit the white belly from anus to head and clawing the organs out and ripping the stiff, red gills up to the jaws pulled everything out and winged everything except the stomach into the tall snake-grasses.

He scraped the black blood from the sac along the spine at the roof of the empty-cathedral rib cage, dropped the fish, the lights of its silvery flanks dulling and going out, into her creel, and cut the stomach open to show us what was in it. The green-black mush contained caddis larvae and some sculpin, their outsized little bull heads and flared pectorals still distinct. Its tiny, dainty feet undigested, its head, button-black eyes and comical ears intact, a baby fieldmouse had also been swallowed by the eating machine.

"Ugh," she said. "Poor thing."

We peered into the mush of corpses in the murderer's cellar of the once-quicksilvery body. With a laugh he threw the stomach inland up over the rocks and splashed up out of the shallows and up over the rocks toward the parking area shouting come on, come on folks, suppertime, come on.

He had too much to drink that evening. A cigarette dripping from his lips, his bourbon making a ring on the piano top, he banged away at chopsticks then some half-forgotten finger exercise. At dinner he downed one glass of wine after another. With milk-pink, horrid eyes he went for her. Poor little fieldmouse, poor little creature of God, poor little mouse-baby. His smile was not real. The unhealthy light glowing around his face was not real. You could feel, like an invisible pike stuck through the air, his need now to hurt someone.

Poor little mouse he leered, poor little fieldmouse door-mouse. She thinks a trout shouldn't eat. A trout shouldn't eat a poor little fieldmouse. Better to starve. Nature should be daffodils and butterflies. No—drawing a finger across his throat to make the snick-sound of a dirk—killing. It was like that. He just singlemindedly (to the extent he knew what he was doing) went for her. He referred to her in the third person, speaking to the world at large of her, describing her squeamishness with a false-smiling, false-reasonable drunk's cleverness from which the sarcasm dripped like honey.

He mumbled and fell silent. Stared at his plate. You could feel it building. He looked up: red pig-eyes. The Hunter I knew was not present. Poor little doormouse he informed whomever it was he thought he was talking to, she's sorry for the poor little fieldmouse, the doormouse is sorry for the fieldmouse.

He wondered, out loud, if she had ever seen a squad of terrorists take a village. He wondered, making his inquiry of the general air, if she knew how children screaming in a burning desert schoolhouse sound.

It was cunning. Molly King had led a sheltered life. He was getting at her from really quite a good angle. I saw why the son lived in New Zealand. A couple of people got up and left the table. He fell silent, staring at his plate, his face Mars-red as he waited for it to start to build. Then he was mumbling—it grew—poor creatures, how horrible, a trout shouldn't eat. Poor little mouse, such a hard life . . .

She sat there and took it, her face drained of color. We made it through dessert. Then he was wandering around out in the front hall. We finally got him up to his room. As we were getting him up the steps he addressed, deliberately in his drunkenness, Molly and me. "What a monster," he said of himself half to himself, "how horrible, wants to relax, what a terrible person, what a monster to want to relax . . ."

We got him on his bed on his stomach. He went to sleep with his hands folded under his cheek and one side of his face squashed into the pillow and his soft white hair wisping upon the pillow and, to my surprise, a peacefulness coming over his features as he lost consciousness, his face sliding into an expression of beatific repose.

ten

Molly King stood still, no part of her moving as she stared, forty feet upstream, at the rise of a feeding trout.

I stepped with care through the morning grasses so as not to disturb her.

"One's working," she said. "There."

"I can see it," I said quietly.

"It comes up just every couple minutes."

"OK," I said. "Let's see you catch it."

I watched her wait, with the icy beauty of a heron, for the riseform to show again on the stream's drift.

We had parted awkwardly in the upstairs hallway the night before. I had started to talk about how tired he must be and how much he must have on his mind. And ghosts mustered in her look. Her brows lifted, not pleasantly, and the light of ten generations came into her eyes. Senators and generals of cavalry were looking out at me. With a shiver I realized I was not to speak of it. I was not to mention it. I was not to make excuses for him. We said goodnight and turned from each other in that narrow corridor and I went to my room and lay awake tossing, seeing the haughtily lifted chin and those ruling, enslaving eyes.

Now in the morning light as I watched her line lay down smooth as the swipe of a bricklayer's trowel as she delivered her fly to the waters, the feeling was as real in me as it had been by night. I was under her spell.

Waiting for the fish to rise she addressed me sidelong:

"Can you see it?"

"Yes," I said. "It's right where it's been. Try again."

She cast again and caught it. Her expression broke into a smile and the arc of her rod trembled against the sky and she stood, turned at the waist, rod on high, gazing down at the fish where it struggled in the water as a goddess might follow with aloof fascination the contortions of a fate-snared mortal.

She waited. It stopped fighting. She drew it to her.

"Big trout in Alaska," I said.

"That's what I hear."

"You must be excited."

"I am."

She unhooked it and let it go, wiping her hand.

"Your father's going to miss you."

She considered this. She was getting her leader smoothed out and her fly spruced up. She stood in the current looking down at her equipment as she worked with it, a wan smile on her lips.

Suddenly she reeled in. She hooked her fly to her rod.

Wading to where I was standing on the bank she stood in the water looking up at me, a question on her face I thought, though with those glasses it was hard to tell.

"You know him," she said. "What do you think he'll do?"

I thought he'd probably be fine and I said so. It didn't seem to be what she wanted to hear. She frowned. Climbed from the water.

Walking past me in her boots she went to a grassy rise, sat, lay her rod down and took her hat off.

She had walked past me without a word, knowing I would know I was invited to follow. If I hadn't it would have mattered no more than if a taxi she had phoned failed to arrive. She sat on that plush rise of grass with a booted leg drawn up and her ankle held in both hands. Her hair fell beside her cheek as she gazed out over the water, and I was looking at her. She was the high priestess of herself. She couldn't help it. I went over and sat by her.

The water poured and slid along before our eyes.

She took her dark glasses off and lowered her head, waiting for me to tell her something wonderful.

I was watching the water, then I felt her turn and look at me. Suddenly she was talking—without preparation, as if a play had skipped a scene. She told me of mile-long swims with him when she was growing up, of his great energy—the stallion he'd broken at the dude ranch they'd visited one summer, and how he would sit in his study into the small hours of the morning with a mug of coffee by his elbow, his sleeves rolled up and his forehead in a hand as he went through the communiqués and white papers he'd brought home with him.

She spoke of her mother. Joan King wasn't well—nothing so

drastic as to require her going to a place of care but neither was it the mere eccentricity Hunter kept trying to pretend it was. In the shadows of the high-ceilinged rooms of the old house Joan would swoon for days into a kind of torpor, scarcely eating, an arm trailed over the arm of her chaise, her head thrown back, talking to herself, whispering, recounting, in a voice dry as desert winds, things that had happened and things that had not.

The day was becoming hotter, the atmosphere more dense, the humidity unpleasant suddenly.

She remembered her mother as a young woman. The dreaminess had been there—a certain fay, side-sliding absent-mindedness—but nothing serious, nothing to call sickness. Then Hunter began to be away from home. Molly watched the change start to take place in her mother. She told me all this in a matter-of-fact tone as we sat there, so strangely side by side, watching the stream.

A breeze blew our hair. The sky above the next valley was lavender. When our shoulders happened to touch she didn't seem to notice. I was hearing now about a trip they'd taken, a trip abroad—at twelve and fourteen Molly and Peter had travelled with their mother to England. One evening driving a country road they passed, at a distance, a lovely little village, quaint inns and shops nestled into a gentle hillside gleaming golden in the faroff sunset. "Oh," her mother had said. "Look at that. They must be so happy there." She seemed to be speaking to herself, her voice as dreamy as the sight, drifting away from them as they drove, of the faraway village. "They must care for each other there," Joan King said. Dutifully Molly and Peter sat straight and craned their necks to see. They could catch only a glimpse of the little town's cluster of roofs speeding away in the coming dusk. "They must all care for each other," Joan was

murmuring to herself, "and come if they need each other, and stay by each other, and love each other."

Molly sat straight, stung by the memory. I turned to look at her. I was inches from her. She did not cry. Looking out over the water she just lifted a hand and brushing, with her fingers, her hair from her eyes set her jaw.

That was brave. The smooth long nose, the sardonic smile that was not a smile, ruined me. Staring out over the water she knew it. The air whirled as heat and blasts of sudden cool flew about us. Then she did turn. She looked at me. There was a slight, interested light now in the gunmetal eyes.

I was lost. As a favor, I suppose, she placed a hand against the back of my neck as we waited to see what we would do.

She shut her eyes when I kissed her.

For long seconds we tried that kiss out. It was endless. Drink of pain-cold water after trail-miles of dust. I don't know what it was. Our faces moved apart. She didn't take her hand from the back of my neck. Her eyes were looking my face up and down, that hand lightly staying where it was against the back of my neck as her eyes roved the features of my face.

"Should I stay?"

Should she cancel Alaska. I wasn't prepared for that. Should she stay here and have an affair with me. I could see my eyes reflected in the shadowed parks of her eyes. She wanted to see how this would feel. She wanted to see if I could surprise her. She was very beautiful as we gazed at each other, her fingers lightly, firmly against the back of my neck. It was impossible.

I turned—swerved. I fled. I had seen the hook. She must have felt the change. Her hand went away. We turned from each other as the storm air blew against us and here he came, gesturing, waving impatiently at us as he tromped onward through the high grasses. There was the stream he pointed, there was the water for God's sake, *there*—what were we waiting for? What was wrong? Why weren't we fishing?

We got to our feet. He was hung over. He came striding up, boots flopping, equipment rustling and clicking, battered hat pulled low. The eyes were a weary pink. You could see, in the grim set of the big face, that he was willing himself to be energetic. The light in his eyes was low yet it was there, burning through his exhaustion.

By the minute the storm air tightened.

"Well we're here to catch fish aren't we? So let's catch some. Let's catch us a fish."

He spoke without looking at us, walking past us to the stream's edge as if afraid one of us might say something he didn't want to hear.

He was going to organize us. His equipment swinging from him he went to the water's edge and with his back to us stood scanning the currents.

"Don't you want to catch a fish Moll? Hm? Isn't that the point? Catching fish? Doesn't she want to catch a fish?"

Getting a grip on herself (you could see it—it was like a hydraulic press compacting an automobile down to a cube) she kept her expression impassive.

"She wants to catch a fish," he said to himself as he looked the currents over. "She wants to catch a fish Joe. Don't you Moll?"

"Yes," she said.

"Well there he is, there's your fish, right there."

"I see him," she said.

She watched the riseform disappear, then turned and went

and got her rod. She would be his little girl for him this last time. The rumble tumbled over itself and after a second's silence there was a crack and flash and again the diminishing, deep-throated grumbling of the summer storm as it marched down the next valley.

Upstream of us yet another expanding circle was smoothing out and disappearing on the gliding gray.

"What've you got on?"

"This."

She showed him.

"That's too big. Here."

He took her fly box from her to look through it.

"I wonder," I said, "if it's the same one you caught earlier."

"The one what?" he asked annoyedly.

A terrific, purple blackness.

"Here," he said.

He tied it on for her.

The bruised storm clouds rumbled eastward down the next valley illumined by explosions of lighting, as if a war were going on.

"What is it?" I asked.

"Keep it soft," he whispered to her as she ventured into the water. "Make sure you've got enough slack. You've got a change in current, right there, see?"

She nodded and made her cast, the water eddying around her boots, flowing at her and around her and on downstream of her through the three stone arches of the bridge.

"That's going to take the fish Moll. No. All right. Your float wasn't right. Get it more to the right, in toward the bank at an angle—see?"

His face was gray.

There were many small circles now on the current, disappearing even as they formed.

"Don't rain," she said.

He squinted at the mountain.

"It shouldn't be too bad. It's going east. Set your hook for God's sake Molly you've got a fish."

It was raining. I tilted my hat against it. She was leaning down to free the pattering trout. He turned his collar up, fumbling for a cigarette and turning from the rain to light it.

She stepped upstream away from us, her back wading away from us as she cast her fly into the dripping grasses that grew along the bank, with a rod-twitch flicking it back out of the grasses and down onto the water as if a delicious beetle or ant had fallen in.

He watched her, cupping his cigarette.

"That's going to take a fish," he said.

One struck but she missed. She moved on upstream aiming short, deft casts at the rise-rings among the circles the raindrops made on the current.

"Cast there again," he called.

"Where?"

"There."

"Like that?"

"Yes," he coughed.

He was coughing. He didn't sound good. He turned and, bent, fist to mouth, watched her out of the corner of an eye and coughed. Here it came.

"Strike!" he yelled. "Missed him. That's all right there's another, to your left, right there."

The rain had lightened and it was possible now to see down into the water. I watched the dark arrow that was the trout, its tail-fin wagging suavely, angle up to drift with her fly, looking it over.

"He's interested," he said. "He's interested Moll—"

The answer was no. With a swirl it returned to its feeding slot and lazed there, pectoral fins flowering, the curves of the trout's moving fins flowing with the curves of the stream's currents as the water flowed over the fish toward us.

She waited, giving her quarry a rest, then carefully cast to it again but some unknowable factor wasn't correct and her presentation put the trout down.

She waded on upstream, casting as she went. He walked after her along the bank, watching. Then he stopped, standing with his hands on his hips.

She had one on now and holding her rod high in a sunny final flurry of drops was fighting it. He was shouting instructions out over the water to her but busy with the trout she seemed not to hear. She had it netted and was turned toward us, holding it up.

"It's a beauty Moll!" he shouted.

Bending down she saved its life.

We watched her work her way up through a stretch of riffles. But for her long-visored hat I wouldn't have known who the tall figure was in the distance flicking sharp licks of short-float casts onto the splashing currents.

The rain came again in a hiss, the air going all gray. Through the rain we watched her move up into the long, broad pool that lay above the riffles. I looked at him. His face was mild as he gazed out over the water, his eyes gentle and sad.

Standing at a distance in the rain she worked to rig with a nymph and then, rod readied, was casting in the curtaining summer shower. As her weighted fly tumbled downstream over the bottom turning at the waist she swung with each drift like a matador with a cape.

He watched her.

A miniature angler at a distance in the rain's blur she cast her way on upstream through the faraway flat of the pool. We stood watching her. Above the pool, going behind some trees, the stream turned a corner.

She went around it.

She was gone.

Empty, the stream flowed through the meadow in the swaying, curtaining rain.

Droplets hung from the brim of his hat.

I asked him if he wanted to keep on fishing.

He looked at me out from under the brim of that hat with exhausted eyes that even in their hungover uncertainty held a wonderful, innocent light—that spark, that vulnerability—that I shall never forget.

He reminded me of a little boy in his slicker and too-big hat fallen off his bicycle for the hundredth time and tired and discouraged but ready to get back on and try again.

"I'm game," he said.

So we fished. But it was no good. He was tying his knots with trembly hands. We nymphed our way upstream, he fishing the right bank, I the left. We fished for half an hour, each catching a trout. The weather cleared completely, a last shower spattering down and between breaking-apart white clouds the distant, high vault of the true-blue sky appearing. With a twist he had the little fish he'd caught freed. But he was shaking his head. He looked terrible. He said he was going back. He turned and struggled up the bank, water pouring down him, his broad back—net hanging down—sagging as he went away across the meadow.

Columns of gold poured from the clouds, dramatic shafts of light like the broken pillars and pilasters of some ruined heavenly city.

There was a newness, in that light, to the glittering pools and runs.

Hugely the sun's rays slanted from the clouds, the after-rain light winking and dancing blindingly on the water where the stream wound away through the meadow. The late-summer cornfields were a deep green on the foothills to the south, and above the rolling hillsides of corn the miles-long, straight, towering Pennsylvania mountain went away into the west with chalk-white clouds blowing across.

He was going to offer his services as a super-consultant, a specialist in high-level international lobbying. He was agitated, smoothing his hand again and again over his bald dome and down the circlet-mane of white hair, coughing, speaking into his glass as he drank, holding his smoking cigarette away from his eyes, telling me of prospects, contacts, stratagems—the expertise "I bring to a thing like this—"

He took a gulp of bourbon, grizzled pinkie extended, eyes wide. Frowning he rapped his glass down *bam*.

He was flying to San Juan the following morning. A real estate syndicate—his hand slid out for his cigarettes—wanted to come up into Georgia. They wanted advice. Leaning forward, cupping a hand around his lighter, drawing his Camel to life with hooded eyes. Wanted to start buying in Florida. Wanted to—he looked at me. So as to. He looked surprised. He couldn't think of the word he wanted. He blinked at me.

Fluttering his cigarette hand he looked down, trying to force his brain to search. In order to, he said. He was embarrassed. In order to. Evolve. Evolve into it. Evolve. He had found the word. He seemed to shrink and would not look at me as he continued to talk, giving me a little lecture now on regulatory climate, as if rehearsing what he would say tomorrow in San Juan.

He was at the Club every weekend. He was traveling, reactivating old contacts and cementing new ones, lining up work, ever just off a plane or about to get on one. But at week's end, no matter where he was, he would always come back, even if it meant crossing an ocean, to spend at least part of Saturday and Sunday up at the Club fishing.

He didn't look good. He was pushing himself. He was in the unending hurry of a man trying to avoid admitting there is no longer any reason to hurry. There was something he had to accomplish. I don't know what it was. I don't think he did, it was just there, pushing him. No time, no time . . .

I sat with him one evening and listened to a flurry of predictions for the economy of the American Southwest. When he paused and I opened my mouth to ask a question he started talking again before I could get a word out. His plaid shirt was buttoned wrong, each button buttoned one buttonhole below the correct one, the right collar tilting up almost to his ear as he sat slouched, jiggling his drink, looking at it as the words poured from him.

I started to hear scattered memories. Hints of fears came out, just hints. His feelings about his career, enemies he'd had, accomplishments he was proud of, his abiding love of the outdoors. He described, disjointedly—the powerful hands floating unneeded in the air, his tears under the stars, how unbelievably clever the Treasury Secretary could be, his child's terror of the dark and what his father had said to him sitting there on the edge of his bed that time. How the stream had looked more beautiful that first June morning than he'd ever seen it, the forest washed fresh by the previous evening's rain and the wilderness shining all around him as he stood looking out through the trees at their silvery bodies waving in the current. I felt I was glimpsing, through small cracks beginning to appear in his armor, his true self—human, confused, vulnerable—or what would have been had he been able in his life to let it out . . . he seemed to like me. Sometimes though as I listened to him that autumn I'm not sure he knew who I was as he sat there jiggling the ice in his glass and wandering from unfinished thought to unfinished thought.

One evening I finally had to excuse myself. I think he would've talked into the small hours of the morning if I'd let him. He gave a curt nod when I made my excuses and got out of my chair, not looking at me but staring across the room and nodding, once, in silent admission that he would not have been able to listen anymore either, nodding just that once, the weather-cured face stoical, the eyes holding on, sad and dim as he looked out over the room, and I left him sitting there with it and went up to join my family.

Marian had met me at the door to our house in the rain when I arrived back home after that last time with Molly. We didn't say anything. I'd left the Club early and driven straight home through the day's squalls and sudden bursts of sunlight, and as I came up the walk she was at the door in her favorite sweater. She needed to know what only I could tell her. I answered the question she'd decided not to ask by taking her in my arms and holding her. We held each other, the rain falling on the lawn behind us through the open door and our embrace tight and growing tighter as we stood there, and gently I scratched the back of her head, which she likes, until from the rear of the house a crashing of chairs and the pulsing of battery-driven death rays plunged us forward into the rest of what I hope will be a quiet, fine life.

Sean was still fighting in school and could still be wary of me but this would pass. Richard—a comedian—I can hardly wait to see turn out. The man of the house I refer to as Your Average Joe—I like Joe better than Joseph. I'm a good news-paperman, a good father, an OK Joe. I have my health. I have the good fortune to be married to Marian. There really isn't anything, when I take a step back and look at it, that I want that I don't have. I'm satisfied. If that makes me dull, I'm dull.

He was my opposite, an intriguing, impossible person, never at rest. He told me about the fish—I'm sure I'm the only one he ever told. He told me how he went up there time after time, climbing the hard climb to the rock-guarded pool again and again—it was lonely. I think he liked that. I think other people were hell for him. I don't know. I don't know about such a fish. I don't know about a trout that size. I'll never see such a fish.

Do you think enough rose-bellied cutthroat, flashing to take your fly on those fast western streams, can equal—by whatever arithmetic—what surged out of the mirrory darkness that first June dusk?

I think so. I think small fish, simple memories, can be enough.

eleven

Peering down he thought he saw a way to descend. He was on his hands and knees looking down, studying the thirty-foot cliff, a facewall of rock slabs and shelves, with wizened plants rooted in crannies, that plunged to the swift main current below. Leaning out over the drop he thought he saw a way to climb down to a vantage point from which, awkward though it would be, he would be able to cast effectively to the seam between the swift current and the slower water of the pool where food would be tumbling out of faster water into slower and it might, somewhere deep, be watching.

It would be exhausting work and he relished the thought. Thirty feet directly below his eyes the current coursed past the rock wall like many bunched dark backs of racehorses surging.

Half-sliding, stone scratching his skin, elbows out, hands

holding holds, a booted foot pawing in the air for a ledge, he struggled down. Then he was standing—panting—on an underwater ledge twice as narrow as his feet. He edged sideways, feeling with his boots-feet for more ledge—a step came down on water, no rock, no ledge, no bottom and he almost
went.

Saved himself by grabbing a handhold of rock and holding it for slipping, terrifying seconds until he could find a heelhold and quickly using that get a better handhold. The current swung him around face-first into the wall of rock like a wind-slammed door.

Water poured into his boots. He rested, stream water pouring down him, sweat pouring down his face, secret satisfaction and pleasure flickering. Managing in the coursing current to worm and contort out of his boots, empty them, drape them, backwards, around his neck like the mantle of some ignominious honorary degree and haul himself grimly back up the cliff, he took his hat off. He took off his vest. He peeled his shirt off and wrung it and spread it on a rock, sorted his soggy equipment, hung his boots over a branch, and sitting on the edge of the cliff and swinging his legs ate a plum.

It was hot. A breezeless hundred. He sucked at the fruit. He could've drowned, could've died. Moist, cool, sweet. Lavender-gold. By some miracle his rod had survived. Sucking noises he winced. Tart-sweet. Saw himself go under forever. With boots full like that. Not a chance. Juicy. There were worse things than drowning. Giving up was worse. He winged the pit into the woods. He got up and went into the cool of the forest and set about stripping the shaggy, tensile vines from where they wound around the treetrunks and hung from the branches and scurried, like fuses, along the forest floor. They made begrudging, ripping sounds as he tore them from where they lived. Trees and people and streams were to be made use of. He was a conservationist, had contributed generously to the cause, served on boards and been strong in helping good bills get through Congress. But it was the magnanimity of the victor, the fairness-instinct of the conqueror. Nature is there for us to use so it's in our interest to keep the natural world healthy. Roughsplicing the vines into a line he fashioned of one end a harnessbelt. The other end he made fast to a tree. Paying his vine-rope out through a hand he lowered himself down the facewall, found places for his feet, tied what slack remained into a modified tautline-hitch, and, testing, let go.

Hanging suspended, leaning out halfway down the cliff wiping the sweat from his eyes with a forearm, he precariously got his rod ready.

He made his cast, the bristly, swept-back collar of his Muddler Minnow settling down on the crease between fast water and slow and the big fly sinking quick. When he thought it was where something might be waiting for it he gave it a tweak, his rodtip bobbing and straightening and his fly, thus, making an intriguing little dart, down where the light does not reach.

His entire body, poised, heels dug in, torso leaning out from the cliff-face, was a single-minded nerve waiting—straining—to feel the hit.

He tried the same cast again without result. With difficulty he squirmed into a different position, trying that way. He slid back to his first position again. He tried different patterns, weights, leader lengths and thicknesses, his eyes peacefully empty as he worked, the sun-leathered forehead unwrinkled, the chapped mouth calm as he concentrated on what he was doing. The sun was low now but the day's heat still hung, oven-hot, over the mountains. To the east above the treetops two were circling, their black, serrated wings set wide as they gyred up the invisible pillar of rising ground-heat.

The forest had fallen quiet with the first thinning out of the day's light. A stray breeze brought pine smell to his whistling nostrils. He remembered his boyhood, the stretching summers, how he would hike untired for miles out of the city into the July meadows to the secret, glittering brook where his hoppers and pincered hellgrammites sent the wild trout mad.

He remembered swimming from morning 'til sunset in the waters of the quarry and how the summer he whipped his block's bully, the others pressing around them as they pummelled each other in the August dust, he had felt like a champion until, his mother discovering the caked blood on him when he came into the cool of the house, he was told he should not play with such people. He would be going to boarding school soon. There would be a different type there. He remembered stealing ice cream, scooting behind the marble countertop in the shadows of the sweet shop. He remembered his first bike, his first glove, and how in the wintertime his parents would take him skating, the snow plowed back in drifts and bonfires crackling in steel barrels on the immense dark expanse of ice, his parents and he touring gracefully, as if weightless, in and out of the slower others, the three of them skating in magisterial circles, as if life were like this, pride filling him as he swayed left, right, left over the frictionless smoothness in the days when it had seemed there was no end to it.

They were still there, the widespread wings circling silently in the distance against the evening sky.

twelve

It was a good time in our lives. Marian and I were happy in our routines, happy in each other and the boys. Life doesn't stay one way long but that late summer and fall our days were serene. Our careers were going well. Sean liked first grade. He seemed to be getting over his fighting urge and was starting to show signs of being well coordinated. At the soccer games he played in he was collected and slow, waiting, amid the colorful confusion of older boys' jerseys, his chance. He would stand still, bareheaded, for two seconds, three seconds, while the others excitedly never quite had control of the ball—he would be very still, watching the ball. Then seemingly without acceleration, as if motion were the same as rest, he would be in it and would have the ball.

I was proud of him. I took him down to the ponds and

again, because I so badly wanted him to want to learn to fish, I paid no attention to him.

It was trying to burrow out of the light back into the black earth but I had it. It came out of the dirt silently screaming against the light in its writhings. I carried it, not giving Sean a look, to the pond's edge. It plopped in and dancing in squirms around itself was immediately surrounded by fish.

Sean stood watching. I could feel him. I didn't say a word. I walked back, nonchalant, to my worm mine. I scrabbled for one, lost it as its slimy coils spasmed—shudders of oleaginous contraction passing over its body, burrowed for it and had it. I carried it back to the green still and threw it in.

One got it with a slam and there were trout-shadows now lurking and milling in the depths.

"Can I throw one?"

Trying to keep the excitement out of my voice I said "Sure," and we went back to my worm mine. Our fingers chased after them in the soil. Solemn and fascinated on his knees in the grasses as he grabbed for them, he was separate from me. I could feel him, not an extension of me, his own person in his hat. We dug, side by side. I couldn't know what he was thinking. The sense of my own son beside me digging for worms, his skinny knees getting dirty, was wonderful, a feeling more warm than lonely yet a little lonely all the same.

I held mine in a fist and let Sean throw his. He winged it sidearm. The water broiled and was still. I gave him mine. He flipped it in just at our feet, jumping backward when they came roiling up.

They glided back down, circling deep, barely visible, waiting in the murk, glimpses of tail—an eye, flash of bright-spotted side . . .

When I said we should be getting back for breakfast he was reluctant to leave, and because I wanted him to want to come back I insisted we go.

A haze hung on the forest, a whiteness out of which trees, paths, outbuildings and the stream itself, half-hidden, appeared like unfinished thoughts.

It was hot. The water was low when I went out on it. You had to come up on them carefully, pushing no waves ahead of you, and be very exact about the cast. Around noon, in the shadows, if you cast to where you had seen the gentling circle they would go after a tiny March Brown.

They were rising in the hardest places to get to, behind logs, under canopies of brush, around corners, down narrow corridors of overhanging branches.

I couldn't catch one. My casting motion was stiff and there wasn't that sense, that confidence, that if you keep your fly wet sooner or later your luck will turn. Some days you don't have it. It just isn't there.

I'd been fishing long hours without success and I was getting tired. I wanted to sit down. I found a place to rest, some pine needles to sit on and a treetrunk to lean back against. It was good to get vest and boots off. I seated myself in the shade and filling it and tamping it and putting a few matches to it got some good blue-hazy clouds of idle thought going.

Looking through the trunks of the trees at the stream I puffed slowly. I was looking out through the trees and out across the water to where a stationary wave, a swift, smooth hump of water beside a half-submerged rock, poured endlessly through itself, throwing off now and again that slight, random splash no one can explain.

I was in a flow.

I was in time. Hours earlier I'd been casting my fly to the first pristine run of the day. Years earlier, sweating, I had stood, wearing the surgical mask they give you, half-outside-myself with fear and love listening to Marian's scarlet shriek turn into the first wailings of our newborn son. Decades earlier I had stood out in the back yard at twilight feeling the scaly hand of my grandfather close over mine as I began to get the feel of the cast.

Riding the bus to school my mind would toy with how it can be now and you are here, now, riding the school bus. Then you're home eating dinner and worrying about your home-work—eating dinner and worrying about your homework is now. And the next time you think about it you're prematurely gray sitting against a pine smoking a pipe and watching, out through the dark trunks and out across the currents, a hump of smooth water pouring through itself. Sitting here drawing on your briar and thinking these thoughts is now, and somewhere there are forty winters, forty springs and summers and falls.

Ceaselessly the waterwave poured through itself, giving off that random little splash, and as I watched I saw—or thought I saw—a second splash, a different splash, a splash within a splash in the standing wave's curl.

I leaned forward, shading my eyes.

There it was.

I saw the bright body flash.

Instantly I was ambitious. I got my equipment on. You never tire of it, of the rhythms of doing it and the surroundings you do it in and what doing it does to you.

I tied a Cream Marietta on and slipped into the current, directing my cast to a point from which I calculated my fly would ride naturally over the standing wave, but the instant my leader touched down my tiny pair of white wings veered crazily. I tried again but my fly was dragging the instant it hit and it shot away downstream, swinging wide and out into the main current.

Sidestepping upstream and making my cast from above, quartering and with a loop and mend, I was able to get the float I wanted.

I was able to get it for about a second.

My dainty white wings touched down on the swift flow and, pirouetting, shot over the standing wave at the wave's exact speed.

The water splashed brightly.

"Hey!" Marian called. "You got one!"

"A nice little one!" I called over my shoulder as I worked my rod at an angle to the fish to keep it off balance.

I was tiring it, guiding it to me, working it to me, easing it to me as she brought Richard to see while Sean pretended to be interested in firing rocks into the forest.

"Dah!" Richard said imperially.

Wide-eyed, he commanded the stream with an outstretched arm.

"Daddy's caught a fish Richie. See?"

"Dah."

I wetted a hand to lift the trout. I lifted the fish into the sun's rays and it was a brilliance of silvers, lavenders, pinks, blues, golds.

"God," she said. "That's so beautiful."

"Bah dah!" Richard annoyedly admonished the stream, which wasn't doing what he wanted it to. He glared at the sparkling currents with dark, innocent eyes as his mother, holding him, marveled at my trout's colors and his brother kept winging rocks at the trees.

Richard was becoming quite the would-be emperor of his environment. With unspecific gestures of command and the syllable *dah* he was forever trying to organize all that he found around him.

"Oh Richie," she said, jouncing him, "isn't it a beautiful, beautiful fish Daddy's caught?"

"No," he said sadly.

He was staring down in exhaustion at the uncooperative waters.

To refresh it I held the trout back in the current's cool. Lifting the fish again I reached into the slow-gulping, pink-white throat and pinching my soggy fly with tweezers felt, with the hook, for the right way to bring hook and fly back out through cartilage, bone, and skin without tearing anything.

I fish only barbless hooks now but then I was using a barb.

Hook safely out, I held the scintillant artwork back down in the water.

The gills began to fan, rhythmically.

"Will it be all right?"

"Sure."

"Dah," Richard said softly.

The little tail moved side to side, the gills working.

That sudden surge—always a surprise—jag of light like what a damaged retina makes you think you saw, and it was gone.

I reeled in and closed up shop and climbed up the bank and we made our way back through the sleepy forest afternoon, Sean finding and throwing rocks, hoping, I think, to be told not to, and Marian walking beside me when the trail gave us room with the would-be emperor of all forests and streams riding in her arms with his chubby arms around her neck and his head of jet-black hair nestled under her chin.

It's a flow. You're in it. You angle against its vagaries without ever making the mistake of thinking you can understand it.

You can't understand it. You can't shoot life and mount it. The perfect stillness after the perfect shot is the deer perfectly dead, lifeless as a universal truth.

For a long time I kept trying to develop a set of precepts to live by, but the rules change, they come out of you. Let it happen. Let anything happen. It's a way of trusting. The rules are in you. Relax, trust them. Cling to your dreams. The angler's truth is the live, fighting fish.

They keep discovering a new basic particle. That's the way the truth is. Truth is a fighting trout which if you're fortunate fate permits you to play, touch—once—the silvery flanks of, and set free.

You can't hunt the truth. You fish for it, catch it if you can, and turn it loose. It's the only rule I know. It's a feel rather than a rule. It's the feel of trusting the cast to the rod and when you miss one not minding and always, after a successful struggle, setting what you've caught free, Sean, Richard, Marian, the fish, yourself and the future and every memory you've ever had, free.

thirteen

His boots soundless on the needles he glides through the dark of the pines beckoned by the rock-walled pool as if drawn down a dream-corridor toward a door, not wanting to reach out, dazedly, for the knob, yet drawn, reaching out, stepping from the trees onto the ledge of rock and looking down, seeing in his mind the great jaws opening, but he is only looking at water, a scattering of yellow leaves turning slowly on the pool's mirrored surface.

Low clouds block the sun in the west. Around him the flame-orange, lemon-yellow and blood-scarlet hills roll off to the horizon like the swells of a storm-heaving sea.

He goes back through the trees and around and down

through the brush to the water, stepping cautiously from the bushes onto the narrow beach. Burning through some moisture in the west the sun sends a strange, bronze light over the mountains.

That light burns, radiant, upon all things. Nothing casts a shadow in it. The pines are not green in it. They are bronze-gold. The water of the pool, the trees, the rolling hills, his face, hands—everything—burns shadowless gold in that pouring light.

The fish rises as a shadow. It lifts without noise, without swirl, without—it seems—moving, its mass simply there, cruel-eyed, the monstrous body spotted like vision-tricks played by a noon sun, the tall tail, alone the size of a good fish, wagging slowly with the massiveness of the thing's weight as it slides to the edge of the faster water and hanging there watches the currents for food.

In a trance he was moving backward the instant it appeared, melting back, gliding back into the bushes. He turns away now to bite off the outsized Rusty Rat he'd been about to try. Building his leader out—scarcely breathing—and down in gauge he ties on a small dry.

Crawling out of the brush on his hands and knees and coming onto the gravelly beach he draws as close to the water as he dares and with the sparest of motions begins waving line out from his wand.

It angles up, gleaming, like an engine of war, to sip something, jaws gaping, gills flaring—his cast is prayerful in that magic light. It's a subtle presentation, his fly touching down on the dark surface just a foot from the thing's jaws.

The float begins. His fly passes over it. He lets the float

come back to him and draws his line off the water carefully to cast again, the fish, as he does so, moving up at an angle to feed.

Sweat-beads wreathe his brow running into his eyes and his heart is going in his chest as he sends his cast out into that incandescent light.

fourteen

The stream had gone quiet. Nothing was showing in the leaf-cluttered current but some suckers, bottom-feeders. Indolently they rooted over the stones and muck. They're slow, ugly grubbers. Now and then as they grazed one would tilt on its side as it fed, showing a flash of white belly like a snarl. I don't know if they do that because they're struggling to dislodge a difficult piece of food or to scare predators away but I find it unpleasant. It makes the stream suddenly uninviting, in addition to which it always seems that when the suckers are out, trout aren't. I'd been at it since noon. I was starting to lose my concentration.

I looked at my watch. We were having dinner with Hunter and I was going to be late. I splashed ashore and hurried back, though as it turned out I needn't have rushed. He wasn't even in off the stream yet. I had time for a leisurely shower and a shave.

Then Marian and I were sitting under the great beams sipping our drinks.

She had a tricky case coming to trial and I wanted to hear about it. I love hearing about her work—the workings of the law fascinate me. We'd talked about this one before and now she brought me up to date, then we were talking about whether she might want to see if she could work out an arrangement with her firm that would enable her to go part-time—three days a week if they'd go for it. She wanted to be with Richard more, though he likes his daycare-lady fine, and with my promotion it looked like we could get by with her earning less—I started to look at my watch and she asked if Hunter and I had set a time to meet.

I said we had. Six. I looked at my watch. It was twenty after. We finished our drinks. When I checked my watch again it was six-thirty. We looked at each other. I went out to the front hall, looked in the register, and found his room number. I went up to his room and when I knocked the door swung open.

On the dresser the business papers he'd brought with him stood in a stack next to a silver-framed photo of Molly. One of his plaid shirts hung over the back of a chair. His deck shoes, polished and comfortable looking, stood side by side at the foot of the bed, and on the gloss of the floor by the closet lay a pair of handweights.

It was very quiet. The fly buzzing where it had gotten trapped behind the white window-curtain seemed a part of that odd stillness as I walked—I don't know why—to the dresser. I stood looking down at his personal things where they lay strewn beside her photo. His wallet was there, and an un-opened pack of cigarettes. There were keys and some loose change and in the pool of nickels and dimes a lure, an old spoon, the classic "Daredevil," hooks gone, wavy white stripe against a scarlet background faded, chipped by time and by his fingers—I imagine—in the darkness of his pocket smoothing the charm in the hearing room and at the cabinet table, touching for luck what he had owned brand new when summer's roads had carried him out of the city into the endless countryside miles . . .

I went downstairs carrying a floating feeling and said I thought I would just go out and take a look. I went out to the parking area and got into our four-wheeler and drove up the branch-blocked, rutted road as fast as I could drive. I parked and got out and struggled uphill through the thick cover and as the rock-walled pool came into view through the trees I didn't at first understand, in that fierce light pouring out of the west, what I was seeing.

It looked as if he'd decided to lie down and take his ease while he fished, reclining on his side propped by an elbow like some Roman oligarch.

His back was to me. I spoke his name. I moved forward, calling softly to him. Then I was beside him loosening the collar, making sure the air passage was clear, laying him down on his back, stripping my shirt off to make a pillow. His face was like ash. He looked up at me with watery, ruined eyes. He was holding his rod. I tried to take it from him but he gripped it, wouldn't let me have it.

"Caw," he said.

He looked disappointed. He was confused. His lips, a terrible, livid purple, moved tortuously as he tried to get them to speak.

"Cawwww—"

His eyes slid toward the water. I turned and looked. His line was not slack where it entered the pool.

"Cawwwww—"

The eyes were a shallow glaze. They were trying to understand what had happened to them but they couldn't understand—he wanted to say the word he was trying to say. The blue eyes were trying to gather their energy but they couldn't—it wasn't there. It didn't make sense. He wasn't what he'd been.

"Yes," I said feeling as if I were speaking, and moving, in a dream, "you caught it. Now lie back. Take it easy."

I said: "Lie quiet. I'm going to get help."

His rod fell with a clack against the gravel, though he was still holding onto it. I fled down the mountainside falling, picking myself up, tearing down the thick-wooded hillside slapping at branches as they slapped at me and I slammed into the front seat feeling my heart pounding in its cave. I drove wildly. I ran up the steps and burst into the high-ceilinged room in my undershirt shouting.

We phoned for the medics. Gerry Sierra had his bag with him. I drove him back up the mountainside. We got out and beat our way up through the forest but we were too late. He was on his back on the stones as I'd left him. His rod had fallen from his hand. It lay on the stones. The light in the eyes, as they gazed, hardly seeing, up at the pines, was draining away.

He lay crumpled, his hands clawed, the sun-blotched head defenseless where it rested on the pillow I'd made of my shirt.

His lips opened.

The eyes still saw but the light in them was very faint. There was practically no life left in his body but a glimmering, weakening light still shone in the eyes, just at the pupils' centers. He was looking up at the forest, staring up, scarcely aware, at what he could no longer have.

The light went out. Gerry kept trying. The medics were shouting to us up through the trees and I shouted back, my voice odd-sounding inside my own head.

Gerry got to his feet.

The medics burst from the forest. Getting information from us as they worked they tried all that it is their responsibility to try. We closed his eyes. They got the body on a stretcher and didn't need to be gentle with it as their bobbing lights went away into the forest.

Gerry followed them. I was staring down at his rod, a shadow on the stones.

I picked it up, brushed—I don't know why—the dirt from the cork handle. When I lifted the line was tight, running into the blackness.

Then he moved. I felt him, the line moving evenly through the water as he swam against me.

He was off. The rod bobbed as it straightened. The line lay slack now on the flat water in the darkness.

Gerry Sierra's voice came calling to me through the trees and I shouted that I would be right there.

I haven't gone back. I suppose it's still there. Maybe some evening someone will discover it and fish for it. Maybe they'll catch it. I don't know. I don't go up there.

Molly flew back for the service and I spoke briefly with her. Her hair was shorter and she wore it brushed straight. It looked great. It made her look not quite so stylish. She looked wonderful, said Alaska was wonderful. Her face shone with an interested, new light as she told me of the fishing, the people and the towns, touching my arm as the line of guests jostled me forward and now I was shaking hands with a somehow rather unpleasant man sporting a tank-commander's moustache and grinning at me with familiar arctic eyes as he brusquely thanked me for coming and next—last in line—a tall figure, bent, face hidden under a veil, that as I took its pale hand made a sound that had it been loud instead of scarcely audible would have been a keening.

I wanted to write about him, to try and capture him for you, but I don't think I've succeeded. Somehow I feel I never really knew him. He was a difficult man, a man of secrets—The Trickster. He knew how to have fun but I'm not so sure he liked himself. Maybe he did. I don't know. I think there was a wound in him, a secret, broken heart. I don't know why I think of it as a wound but I do, some moonlit beauty trapped in him, something silvery and mysterious and sad lodged deep in him like the broken-off blade of a lance. He was sensitive to the mountains and the flowing waters and he wanted to be sensitive to people too but something prevented it. Something trapped it, and—trapped—it became a wound shining in him, a wound no one must ever touch or discover.

Deep down, he trusted no one.

He could enjoy himself. For short periods he could forget and relax and then it took him, the need, the compulsion, to control. He was tough, yet in him was the wound, the voice in the water, a music he couldn't quite hear and couldn't ever quite stop hearing.

I wanted to describe him for you, to evoke him so you'd—so I'd—understand. But I haven't. I haven't done it. I've lost him. I wish there were something final now that I could say, something to tie it up neatly in a pattern. But that's not possible. I have to let go. I have to let him go now.

fifteen

The fish are thinking.

Stationed in their feeding slots in the current they don't need to look at one another—can sense each other's position by the strange, interflowing telepathy of the communal organism that they are, scattered out across the stream under the water.

It takes place in a flow and is a holding and a continuous repositioning of themselves, hydrodynamically, in relation to the flow, a realigning of themselves reflexively—subtle adjustment of their eight perfect fins, the flow ever changing and they ever changing to meet it and thrive in it, the moving water passing around, under, and over them like a perpetual wind.

In their feeding positions the fish are thinking of what sorts of food might be approaching in the curved, shimmery ceiling of brightness above their heads. They are thinking too of the

Upper World—trees, grass banks, sky, a world that appears to them in the glassy ceiling above them in magnified-diminished, shimmying distortion.

The waterflow's curves and random surges come washing over them and the flow is their Time. They are in it. They think principally of food, of spotting and eating it, but they think also of what lies beyond the tremulous, quivery roof of light extending above their heads—the Upper World, down out of which things sometimes drop into the flow and up out of the flow into which, convulsively, things sometimes fly.

Only two things, the fish know, ever rush out of Time to shatter the shimmering ceiling and disappear into the Upper World.

Food does this.

And sometimes fish do.

We are wary. We must flash toward the Upper World to claim our morsels. It is our lot. Over generations we have learned this and must repeat it among each other as we hold, steadily, smoothly dancing our bodies and fins as we face into Time.

If you can eat one big nourishing thing, they tell each other, *eat it and rest. Let dozens of the tinies go by. Rest. Wait. Look.*

Around you is motion and shadow. The Heaven Light is above. It is bright beyond belief. If you should ever make a moment's leap into it you will find it still, suffocatingly dry and garish beyond imagining.

The Parents live in the Heaven Light.

They are tall. Their eyes are black goggles. They bob, spastically—our opposite, weighted down, dragged down by their nets and boxes and keys and chains and locks and bags and sacs and waistcoats and vests and hats and suspenders and boots.

The Parents' wands are the only real thing about them, the only fish-like thing about them. Their wands are lithesome. They wave them over us.

Learn this: sometimes the Parents do not come, but when they do—outsized, tottering, hall-of-mirror-freak mantises wavering and towering in the Heaven Light as they peer down at us and work their willowy wands—they must be paid attention to.

For it is the Parents who bring us our food, which is birthed by them through their wands and offered, at the end of each wand's almost-invisible umbilical, down out of the Heaven Light and into Time for us.

Thus they feed us.

And we must be grateful.

But we must also be patient and always very cautious, never greedy or quick. For the Parents do not want us to snap our food before it has separated from the umbilical. We must always be sure that the morsel we want has disconnected from the wand-umbilical before we go after it. Because if you do eat a food-bit, the big ones tell the little ones, *before it has detached, a slam will take you.*

The Parent pulls on the umbilical and the food, which would've been delicious, rams your mouth's side and sticks there, horribly, still connected to the food-giver wand, and for punishment the Parent drags you into the blinding Heaven Light stillness.

Also know this: the Parents sometimes grow angry. Even if we scrupulously do not disturb the food if we see it is still connected to an umbilical, even if we properly move away and are gulping only food we can see is connected to no food-giver wand, if we make too much noise then in their rage the Parents will slap and splash the Heaven-Ceiling with their umbilicals and unborn food, and we must flee . . .

Something like this, years ago, having ricochetted in my

brain as a fantasy-version of what fish in a stream might be thinking, emerged as what I came to refer to, in the immodest privacy of my secret thoughts, as a great idea for a little essay.

But I never wrote it and it's just as well. It doesn't hold up. Fish feed at night as well as when it's light. They eat not only insects but each other. The whole thing, if you think about it, falls apart. Trout are just that: trout.

They're killers. Trout eat their own kind.

They're graceful, beautiful. But they're murderers. They're cold biologically, cold in their unfriendliness toward each other, cold the way they mate and cold the way they kill. To take a trout on a fly is to trick a killer into thinking it's swallowed a live victim. Hunters of fowl and antlered game are killers of vegetarians. It's the quarry's sociability that brings it into the gunner's sights. The flock of geese swings down out of its flight path because the birds think they've spotted their own kind among the corn stubble. Surging hormones—the buck's version of love—bring it into the crosshairs of the deerhunter's rifle-scope.

To kill a trout is to kill a killer.

And if the angler prefers not to kill, he or she doesn't have to. The crumpled duck cannot be returned to health. The bleeding elk cannot be made whole. The hunter's success, no matter how perfect the kill, is a kill all the same. The shooter stands in solitude following the perfect shot, a dead animal lying at a distance through the trees, the wilderness still.

When the angler scores there is the vibrant life-connection through line and rod to the striving fish, and when the defeated trout has rolled on its side and floated, unresisting, to your net, it may be nursed back to health and released.

To traumatize and exhaust a guiltless fish is no moral achievement perhaps but if you were someone's sport and could choose between being exhausted, revived, and set free on the one hand and death on the other, which would you pick?

When I would try and get Marian talking about such things when we were first dating she would listen carefully and ask intelligent questions. At least in the beginning she would. In time it became clear she didn't understand. Her thinking-finger tapped rapidly, impatiently. It wasn't really that she didn't understand. She understood all right but didn't see how I could spend so much time thinking and writing—or trying to—about questions that haven't any answer. Beyond a certain point she simply couldn't get interested in what fish might think or how hunting and fishing might have essences that differ, and I think she felt that past a certain point I shouldn't be interested either.

"Why do you have to make such a drama out of it?" I remember her asking me one evening shortly after we were married. "Why can't you just do it?"

I don't know. I guess she has a point. At the same time my mind will wander where it will wander and there's not an awful lot I can do about that. Still, for whatever reason my speculative flights are fewer now than they were five, ten years ago. I've been working on some funny little fantasies though that I think I might try to get my boss to let me run. So there—as the English say—you are.

We talk about her work, which fascinates me as I've said, and we talk about friends of ours and about our families and about Sean and Richie and our hopes for them, but if we ever do get on the other we don't stay on it long.

And that's fine—good for me probably. I will never forget

the night I was trying to explain the Möbius strip to her—you know you cut a long rectangle and twist it once then tape the ends together to make what looks like a hoop but isn't?

Our heads huddling in the lamplight I demonstrated, on the one I'd made to show her, how an imaginary little man walking on one side of the strip if he kept walking long enough would walk right onto the opposite side. I could feel her warmth beside me and smell the lemon in her shampoo as we bent toward each other before the lamp.

"See?" I said. "A little man walking goes along this apparently flat surface until . . . see? See how he was up here before and now he's underneath, upside down, walking here on the underside?"

She studied what she was seeing, tapping her finger on my arm.

"But wouldn't," she asked with interest, "the little man fall off?"

sixteen

Casting with the department-store rig I'd purchased was like playing with a toy against the memory-feel of what eight feet of bamboo can do, but my worm-offering plopped down fine. The torquing, pink flesh drifted down in the pond water and there was a streak of light and jerking the little rod up I was fast to a fish.

I could feel Sean standing behind me. I said nothing. Hunkering in the tall reeds at the water's edge I leaned out, holding my rod up, to pull the outraged trout toward me. Twisting the hook I freed it.

The fish shot away. As before, the pond lay still in the sharp morning light.

It was spring, the start of another season.

We stood looking at the water and I was about to go get another worm when he asked if he could try.

I said, "Oh sure." We went and got another big nightcrawler and garlanded our five-and-dime hook with its coils. I stood with him, showing him what to do.

He lifted the visor of his cap to survey the green, sun-bright still. I said chuck it in. With an unsmooth swing he made his cast. It didn't get very far out. The pond swirled. There was a terrific splashing and ruckus. I said "Lift your rod" and he did, and, his line glistening and trembling as the fat trout fought him, with a child's cry of delight he was connected.